"A STINGING COMME[...]
OF FANCY."

"HILARIOUSLY FUNNY."

—*Library Journal*

From **T. H. White**, best-selling author of *The Sword and the Stone*, *The Once and Future King*, and *The Book of Beasts*, comes this long unavailable satirical fantasy of twentieth-century Ireland. First published in 1947, *The Elephant and the Kangaroo* is something of a modern-day *Gulliver's Travels*, exploring an English writer's journey through a land at once familiar and alien, as he answers an Almighty challenge to save a world which he's not sure is really worth preserving. And it doesn't take him long to find out that building an ark just isn't as easy as it used to be. . . .

THE ELEPHANT
AND
THE KANGAROO

THE ELEPHANT
AND
THE KANGAROO

T. H. White

A SIGNET BOOK

NEW AMERICAN LIBRARY

A DIVISION OF PENGUIN BOOKS USA INC.

SIGNET, SIGNET CLASSIC, MENTOR, ONYX, PLUME, MERIDIAN
and NAL BOOKS are published by New American Library, a division of
Penguin Books USA Inc., 1633 Broadway, New York, New York 10019

First Signet Printing, June, 1989

1 2 3 4 5 6 7 8 9

PRINTED IN THE UNITED STATES OF AMERICA

FOR DAVID GARNETT

There is a tide in the affairs of men,
Which, taken at the flood, leads on to fortune;
Omitted, all the voyage of their life
Is bound in shallows, and in miseries.

CHAPTER
I

M r. White was standing in his workshop, or playroom, with his spectacles on the end of his nose and a small oilcan in one hand. He was a tall, middle-aged man, with gray hair and a straggling beard, like one of the Sikhs at Queen Victoria's funeral. He looked willing and faintly anxious, like a good dog who was going to retrieve your walking stick from the sea.

The playroom was full of wood shavings, books, tools, paints, guns, fishing rods, bee veils, etc. It had a plain board floor, unstained, and the bookshelves were plain. There was one armchair and a homemade lathe, which did not work. Some swallows had nested on the door of the tool cupboard, and the four young swallows were sitting in a row in their nest. The yellow slits of their mouths made them look like knights in armor wearing tilting helms made of fluff.

Mr. White had been constructing a secret door in the board floor, where he could hide his gold watch. He had hinged one of the boards invisibly, or fairly invisibly, and one of the nails was a false one, which could be pulled out when he wanted to lift the board. The watch, for which he had made this arrangement, had seven separate dials on its face. It could tell the name of the month, the date, the day of the week, the phase of the moon, the

9

time, and the second. It was also a stop watch for
timing races, and a repeater, for telling the hours,
quarters, and minutes in the dark. There were so
many dials, in fact, that it was difficult to tell the
time by it, and, as it was a full hunter which
needed to be opened by pressing a spring before
it could be consulted at all, the best place for it
was under the floor. Besides, it was valuable.

Mr. White had been oiling the nail.

The female swallow flashed in at the window
with a daddy longlegs, saw him standing between
her and the nest, banked sharply, and dashed out
of the window with a squeak. All the baby swallows shot out of the nest like jacks-in-a-box, with
their mouths wide open, squealing, "Me! Me! Me!
Me!" They meant the daddy longlegs. He thoughtfully put one drop of lubricating oil into each
mouth, and the swallows subsided into the nest,
smacking their lips doubtfully.

This was the moment when the commotion
started downstairs.

Two doors opened more quickly and loudly than
was usual—he identified them as the kitchen and
the back door—and Mikey O'Callaghan's voice said:
"Jesus, Mary and Jo ..." Before it had finished
the "Joseph," it was out at the back. Then Mrs.
O'Callaghan's voice began the rosary on a high
howling note like "whooo." "Houlymerrymotherav-
god ..." There was a noise of metal falling off a
shelf—he thought it would probably be one of the
saucepans—which the Irish aptly call burners—and
then came the breaking of china, which the Irish
call delf. He thought it sounded like cups and
saucers. The next thing was that the rosary came
to a halt in the middle of a "blistartthoumanxtrim,"
the kitchen door banged for the second time, and
Mrs. O'Callaghan came scampering up the stairs,
like a regiment of mice with the cat after them.

She was a tall, thin woman, over fifty years of age, who never stopped working and never got anything done. She used to drop things in the middle and do something else, with disappointing results.

A beautiful red setter called Brownie, who had been asleep in the playroom armchair, woke up at the sound of Mrs. O'Callaghan scampering, and began to bark in a hysterical falsetto.

"Mr. White, Mr. White, there's something come down the chimley!"

"What sort of thing?"

"Like a banshee!"

Brownie, who had recognized the scamperer and decided that a game was to be played, continued to bark and to romp with Mrs. O'Callaghan, which caused them to carry on their conversation in shouts.

"Is it a jackdaw?"

The jackdaws had built in all the chimneys at Burkestown, after first filling them with twigs, so that it was impossible to have a fire in the house after the hatching season, and young daws in the fireplaces were fairly common objects. The tolerant creatures had respected the kitchen chimney, however, and it was still possible to have hot meals. When Mr. White asked if it were a jackdaw, he had suffered a momentary qualm that perhaps this tolerance might be at an end, and that they would have to live on cold ham in future.

"No."

"Is it a cat?"

Some cats had also taken to the chimneys at Burkestown, in the lower parts which were free of twigs, and had gone wild there. They came out at night like Harpies, to raid the dairy and the pantry, but vanished up the chimney if anybody opened the door. Nobody knew what to do about them, as they were smokeproof. It was an interesting example of synechthry.

Mrs. O'Callaghan denied the cats. Her lodger's scientific attitude had calmed her, so that she no longer wanted to recite the rosary for the time being. She was ready to take a defensive interest in what had come down, and even to repel Brownie if she could. Mr. White, always the practical Englishman, was taking control of the situation, as he generally did, and she was willing that he should do so. Her life was made up of baffling situations— for instance, although it was August, her husband was still doing the previous year's ploughing—and her usual reaction to them was to ignore them as much as possible. When Mr. White had insisted on putting up a Wincharger to make some electric light for them, for instance, Mrs. O'Callaghan had refused to learn how to put on the brake, on the principle that if she did not know how to do it then she could not be blamed if it broke because she had not.

She shouted hopefully, like somebody playing a card and wondering what would be played on top of it: "It be's more like a feather mop."

He knew it could not be a mop because he had swept the chimney in the room above, which was dog-legged, and, besides, the kitchen range had three dampers. He opened the door for Brownie, who rushed out under the impression that she was going for a walk, and closed it again resourcefully, so that the unnatural silence smote upon the ear.

"What do you think it is?"

Just like going to the Docther, thought Mrs. O'Callaghan. "Does it hurt here?" "Where do yez feel the pain, Ma'am?" She folded her long fingers together and gave a candid opinion.

"It might be the Archangel Michael."

Nothing could have made Mr. White feel angrier. He had a religious argument with Mrs. O'Callaghan about once a month, in which he explained to her with frightful patience that there was no God at all, but that the universe had been created by spontaneous combustion and had been elaborated by natural selection. He felt so strongly on this subject that he had even gone to the trouble of writing a little booklet for Mrs. O'Callaghan, in which he had explained about Darwin and the amoebae in words of one syllable. But Mrs. O'Callaghan had put it into the clothespress after reading two pages, and Mikey O'Callaghan, whose guiding principle in life was to escape doing work, had used it to light the fire in order to save collecting sticks. When Mr. White had been told about this, he had just turned round and gone out of the room without saying a word.

He generally met Mrs. O'Callaghan praying about twice a day. She used to say her morning prayers in the dining room to the Infant of Prague and her evening rosary in the kitchen, and he would wander in with an oilcan or a hammer, and go out again angrily while Mrs. O'Callaghan gave him a guilty simper. She also went to all the local masses and prayed for an hour on first Friday evenings, as she was engaged upon some sort of marathon novena. He knew, in a way, that the poetry of religion was almost the only piece of color in her life, but he could not help thinking that it was bad for her. He was a serious-minded man and had an uncontrollable wish to stop people doing what was bad for them. As he told Mrs. O'Callaghan repeatedly, prayer was bad for people because it was a kind of wish fulfillment. For instance, said he, if you lose some article or other, you kneel down and pray to St. Anthony to find it for you. But as there is no St. Anthony and no God, as I explained to you in my booklet, these moments which you spend on your knees are moments wasted, which you might have spent in searching for the article. In fact, you are actually doing yourself harm by praying: You are harming yourself just to the amount of the time lost.

Mrs. O'Callaghan was never shocked by Mr. White's religious arguments, but she frequently shocked him. He was always finding out new things that she believed in, such as that angels really flew about on wings or that Jesus Christ really had a beard and a visible halo suspended over his head. He explained to her how big an angel's sternum would have to be, to hold the wing muscles, and bought her a book which contained some fourth-century representations of Jesus Christ, with no beard and no halo. But Mrs. O'Callaghan, though she tried to seem grateful, secretly disliked the book, because, as she pointed out, the pictures were not a bit like Our Lord.

One trouble about these arguments was that he always lost them. Mrs. O'Callaghan had various stonewall explanations which baffled him. For instance, she easily proved that there was a God, however much he talked about amoebae, by showing that God had said there was a God and so there must be. Another of her big guns was about Omnipotence. Whenever Mr. White caught God out in doing something ridiculous or impossible, such as resurrecting the bodies of two cannibals, one of whom had eaten and assimilated the body of the other into his own tissues, Mrs. O'Callaghan would say respectfully: "But we know, Mr. White, that *everything* is possible to God."

However, to get back to the thing which came down the chimney, when Mrs. O'Callaghan stated that it was the Archangel Michael, Mr. White felt a *hysterica passio* or *mother* rising in him.

He said sarcastically: "I suppose it has a halo?"

Mrs. O'Callaghan always took his ironies, and most of his jokes, as plain statements of fact. The result was that he had give up trying to make jokes for her, but he still was unable to cure himself of irony, when annoyed. She now said: "Well, it could be a hat."

Mr. White said with resignation: "I suppose I shall have to find out what it is."

He opened the door—Brownie had been busy scratching the paint off—and placed himself at the head of the expedition, oilcan in hand. Mrs. O'Callaghan fell in behind.

The stairs were covered with oilcloth, and three of the bannisters were broken. On the landing there was a dusty stuffed fox, without a case, whose tail some moths had bitten off, and there were three pots of aged geraniums between the flyblown lace curtains. At the foot of the stairs there was a pastel of Croagh Patrick, which Mr. White had made to commemorate a pilgrimage there, in the days before he became a freethinker.

At this point Mrs. O'Callaghan faintly deserted her leader and drifted into the dining room, where she knelt down in front of the Infant of Prague and prayed for the Archangel to go away.

Mr. White, aware of the desertion, went down the last three steps to the kitchen with a heart that had begun to flutter in spite of him. He opened the door cautiously, in case whatever it was should fly or run out, for he was a man who had been accustomed to keep badgers, hares, rabbits, owls, snakes, foxes, and many other creatures in the house, and he looked carefully round the edge of the door, ready to slam it if necessary.

There the Archangel was, just as she had said, in front of the middle damper.

It hung against the dark background of the range in a nimbus of its own light, looking straight between his eyes, with awful splendor.

CHAPTER
II

After Mr. White had looked at the Archangel for half a minute, he gave a kind of bob or genuflection—"made a leg," as our ancestors used to say—and lifted his hand, as if to take off his hat. Finding no hat to take off, he pulled his forelock in a fumbling way, bowed ungracefully, and shut the door. He went back to Mrs. O'Callaghan in the dining room.

He was intensely annoyed to find that she was praying.

"What's the good of praying to that thing, when you have the Archangel Michael in the kitchen?"

"Is she still there?"

This exasperated him beyond endurance. They had on the farm: one bull who served the neighborhood, a billy goat who stank, a ram, a rooster, two drakes, three turkey cocks, a collie dog, plenty of squeezed bullocks, and two male pigs (no longer entire). Mrs. O'Callaghan referred to all these as "she," either out of modesty or else as a tacit protest against the facts of life.

Mr. White, who was orthodox in his pneumatology, said furiously: "It is not a she, It's an It."

"Then it has me stomach at me."

He put down the oilcan on a plate, to save the sideboard, took the small red paraffin light which burned perpetually in front of the Infant of Prague, and went back to the kitchen. He was afraid of going close to the Archangel, but he put the light on the kitchen table and went out again backward. Perhaps it was the long years of giving mice to owls and flies to swallows and frogs to snakes and milk to hedgehogs, when they came into his possession, which made him do this.

Brownie showed no fear of the Archangel Michael, but went up and sniffed It casually. She immediately lost interest, either because she had no soul or because the Archangel had no smell; it is difficult to be sure which.

When he went back to the dining room, Mrs. O'Callaghan said: "It does be Mikey's fault, the way he was speaking sacrilege of Father Byrne, when he didn't offer us the bullock."

The chief industry of Burkestown was putting the blame on somebody else. Mr. and Mrs. O'Callaghan seldom tried to think about the difficult future—for instance, to think whether it would be advisable to draw home the turf before it got wet again, or whether it might be wise to sow rape in the three acres which were too late for barley —but they were adepts at thinking about the past. When the turf had been left out all winter and most of it stolen, or when the late acres were well covered by a tremendous crop of sorrel, Mrs. O'Callaghan said that the sorrel was Mikey's fault for taking the man to cut potatoes when he might have been working the horses, and Mikey said that the turf was Mrs. O'Callaghan's fault, for buying it at Kilcuddy instead of going to the bog. They were so good at this form of mental exercise that they had got to the stage when they could put the blame on each other before any blame had arisen. For instance, if an inspector came to see the bull's pedigree, Mrs. O'Callaghan would often say, "I gave it to you," before Mikey had time to say, "Where did ye put the bull's pedigree?" Sometimes, when something had been mislaid, they stood opposite each other saying, "It does be your fault, for not putting it in the dresser when I tould ye" or "I did put it in the dresser, but it's your fault for whitewashing the kitchen since," while at the same time holding the missing article in their hands, and even using it to emphasize the points of the argument.

Mr. White said: "We don't know that it is anybody's fault. Perhaps the Archangel has come to praise you, or to give you a message, or as a compliment, or something like that."

"It does be because he was speaking bad about the priests. There was a man in me mother's time (God be good to her) and he tried to drive the priest's bullock off his land with a fork. Do you know, Mr. White, that man was frozen to the clay like a graven statyer on the instant, till they had to get Father Quin from Cashelmor to have him moved (God be good to him)."

"But this has nothing to do with driving bullocks with a fork. All we know is that the Archangel Michael has come down the kitchen chimney, and we shall have to find out what It wants."

"She could be the Devil."

"It could be, but It isn't. We shall have to face It sooner or later, Mrs. O'Callaghan, so we may as well face It now."

"Let Mikey face her, then. He's me husband, isn't he? Running out the scullery door the minute she came down, and leaving his own wife to be torn asunder!"

"I can fetch Mikey if you like. But we all ought to go."

"I won't go a step near her till she's gone."

"But, Mrs. O'Callaghan, you are always saying your prayers and paying for masses and reading

St. Anthony's Annals. I should have thought you would be pleased to see the Archangel Michael. And think what a tremendous thing it is, to happen at Burkestown. Wouldn't you be miserable, afterward, if you had let an Archangel go away from your own kitchen without going to welcome It? If it was only Mrs. James of Ecclestown, you would make her welcome."

"I couldn't go till I have me soul made."

"How long will you take?"

"It might be all night."

"But you can't keep the Archangel Michael waiting all night. . . ."

Mrs. O'Callaghan retreated from the situation by concealing her head in the rosary. Mr. White looked grieved and puzzled for a moment; then, with back and front as either should be, he bustled off to collect Mikey at any rate, like a conscientious sheep dog.

The latter was in the oat loft. He had armed himself with a two-grained fork before hiding there, and, when he heard Mr. White coming up the ladder, he pretended to be turning the oats with the fork. It was August, so there were only a couple of stone of oats left. Mikey had always previously shirked turning them, when they first went in and needed it. Also, a hay fork was scarcely the tool one might choose for turning a heap of grain. However, Mikey was like this.

He was a small, red-faced man of about sixty, who looked a little like the first Duke of Wellington and a little like a tortoise. He had the Wellington nose, and there were folds round his thin neck, so that it looked as if he might suddenly withdraw his head into his shoulders, if menaced. Had he been able to do this, he would certainly have spent the greater part of his life with the head retracted, for he was terrified of almost everything on the farm: of the bull, the horses, the bees, and even of the turkeys. He was nearly always in Mr. White's bad books. This was partly because of his timidity, partly because of his laziness, and partly because he was physically-speaking a kind of Neanderthal idiot. Mr. White was always finding out, with indignation, some new thing which poor Mikey could not do. Although he was supposed to be a farmer, Mikey could not plough, sow, or work horses; but it was not a question of complicated things like these. The things which made Mr. White furious were to him unbelievable. For instance, Mikey could not wind up his watch, or tell the time by the minute hand, or recognize photographs—he used to hold them upside down. Once, when Mr. White took him to Tara to improve his mind, he pointed to Trim steeple, about eight miles away, and asked: "Who's that man?" He did not know his age, nor his own second name—Mr. White had happened to find it for him, on a confirmation certificate, when he was filling up the census forms for the household. He could not work a saw by himself—he used the tip—nor drive a nail. There was a gate in one of his fields which he did not know how to open, so he had to climb over it, pretending that he preferred to do so. Once Mr. White, who was liable to crazes, spent nearly all the winter knitting his own stockings. Somehow he communicated this craze to Mikey, who asked to be taught knitting. For six months, for an hour every evening, Mr. White tried to make him accomplish one plain stitch. He tried with knitting needles and wool; he tried with walking sticks and string; he tried with two pokers and a bit of rope. Mikey sweated profusely through his hands, soiled the wool, and broke one of the walking sticks, but he never made a stitch by himself. It was a grief to him.

The physical imbecility which exasperated Mr. White, and the laziness, and the love of his skin, were imperfectly concealed by Mikey under a veneer of self-satisfaction which he was forced to adopt in self-defense. He tried to believe that he was a handy man, and would sometimes give Mr. White advice about his carpentry, with fatal results. Also, like most weak people, he was liable to become obstinate. To be half-witted and apologetic about it: this Mr. White could have condoned. But to be half-witted and obstinate and self-satisfied, this he could not and would not and did not condone. He never actually abused Mikey, but the veins in his forehead swelled into knots, and he sometimes had to take a dose of Andrews Liver Salt to calm himself.

Mikey O' Callaghan had the local reputation of being simple. This, apart from the peculiarities mentioned, was untrue. At managing the farm he was hopeless enough—that is, at thinking about the work which had to be done—but at thinking how to avoid doing the work, at this he was a genius. One of Mr. White's main annoyances was that he was never sure whether Mikey could not plough for bona fide reasons, or whether he found that not being able to plough was a useful accomplishment, because it saved him from having to do so. Indeed, he sometimes thought that all Mikey's clumsiness and childishness was an unconscious but carefully built defense against having to do work.

What made the situation painful for Mr. White— who suffered much more in trying to improve the O'Callaghans than they suffered in trying not to be improved—was that Mikey was a darling. He was cheerful, affectionate, and kind. He adored Mr. White and would have done anything not to be in his bad books—anything which did not in-

volve work or danger. He was good-tempered,
except when he lost his temper, and this he only
did with inanimate objects, because live ones might
have hit back. Once, when he had shut his finger
in a difficult gate, he was seen to burst into tears
and to kick the gate repeatedly; which hurt his toe
so much that his nose bled, and tears and blood
ran simultaneously from the end of the Punch-
and-Judy beak.

Anyway, Mikey was in the oats loft, turning
about thirty pounds of grain with a two-pronged
fork and trying to look as if it were pretty important to finish it.

"What on earth are you doing?"

"I was getting this turned," said Mikey apologetically. He could see that he was not going to be
allowed to get away with it.

Mr. White looked sarcastically at the fork, swallowed convulsively, and said: "Well, the Archangel
Michael is in the kitchen."

"Oh, Lor!"

"Yes, and if you could do that another time, she
wants you to come in and welcome It."

"Will the chimley go afire?"

"I don't think so."

"Perhaps it would be best," said Mikey sugges-
tively, "if we let him alone?"

"No, it wouldn't be best. There's nothing to be
afraid of. It won't do us any harm."

"Did ye go near him?"

"Yes, twice. It is quite safe."

Mikey had always placed confidence in Mr.
White's word. His admiration now stood the test.
He left the fork in the loft—it was lost for some
weeks after—and came down the ladder, which
Brownie was sadly trying to climb, her eyes fixed
imploringly on her master above. But he was still
frightened. He said pettishly: "Such an hour to

come down the chimley! Why can't they come when it's convaynient?"

Mr. White led his second expedition round the house, to the front door. Somehow he did not want to go by the back way, past the kitchen. They went past the hay barn, which was inhabited by swallows; past the corrugated iron garage, which had Mr. White's motor in it, last driven five years before; past an outhouse known as Ned's House, which had no guttering round the roof and was consequently undermined by damp; past the greenhouse which Mr. White had built, only to find that it was not against a true south wall in summer; past the sundial on which he had sadly painted the motto

They also serve who only stand and wait;

past the necessary house, which had accommodation for two people, side by side; and past the beehives, to which Mikey always gave a wide berth. Finally they ducked quickly in at the front door— quickly, because two swarms of unusually malevolent wild bees had come to live in the fanlight. On hot and thundery days the front door was hardly ever used, for this reason. But it was all for the best, as it saved the linoleum in the hall. There was generally a deep humming in the hall, like a dynamo.

Mrs. O'Callaghan was no longer in front of the Infant of Prague. They could hear her footsteps going to and fro in the bedroom above, where she was changing into her best clothes, to be ready for the Resurrection if necessary. Unfortunately, she was unable to change her underclothes, which she would have liked to do, because the clean ones were in the kitchen cupboard.

She came down in her Sunday best, wearing a

hat. Mr. White thought this ridiculous—which only shows that even Englishmen do not know everything; for Mrs. O'Callaghan was perfectly correct, canonically speaking, in going to meet an Archangel with her head covered, as St. Paul, St. Ambrose, St. Jerome, St. Cyprian, Tertullian, and others have pointed out.

Besides her hat, Mrs. O'Callaghan had an uncorked bottle of holy water, with her thumb over the top. She was ready for the fray.

Like a child going to a party, she was in a twitter.

"Mikey, you're a show! Can't you make yourself nate?"

"Me boots is in the kitchen."

"You want a shave."

"Water?"

To get hot water for shaving, he would have needed to go for the kitchen kettle.

"Well, glory be to God, put on the suit."

While Mikey was changing into his blue suit and clean collar—an act of faith, so far as he was concerned, because the collars were always filthy again by the time he had managed to do them up—Mr. White also went upstairs and put on a tie. He brushed his hair. This had a startling effect on his general appearance, for he seldom brushed it in the usual course of affairs, except when he got up, and seldom wore a hat, and spent most of the day working in the windy garden. The result was that, what with the fluttered hair and the whiskers, his surprised blue eyes were usually like two eggs in a very untidy bird's nest, say a heron's.

When all three were clean and uncomfortable, they formed up in single file and trooped down to the kitchen.

Mrs. O'Callaghan threw about a noggin of holy

water in the direction of the range. Then, as this had no deleterious effect, they knelt down awkwardly in a row beside one of the tables. They did not have to ask questions, or even to pray, but received their instructions in respectful silence. Brownie found a glue pot with which Mr. White had been intending to mend the bannisters, and ate glue rather noisily under the table, while these were given.

CHAPTER
III

There were three other people whose lives were centered round Burkestown at the time of this story, but who were not present during the Announcement. These were: "Master" Pat Geraghty, who was a muddle of Mr. White's; Tommy Plunkett, the general laborer who did all Mikey's work on the farm; and a young, black-bottomed maid of sixteen, whose name was Philomena.

"Master" Geraghty was a compact, middle-aged man with rosy cheeks and bright eyes, who looked the picture of health. Unfortunately, he was a maniac. It was only simple mania, not acute or catatonic, so it passed without comment locally. There were numbers of other lunatics in Cashelmor and its environs, who behaved in a more spectacular way: either by making faces at people over walls, or by indecent exposure, or simply by being locked up for life in a back bedroom. Indeed, a good percentage of the houses in Cashelmor had prisoners in their back bedrooms, some of them strapped to the bed if violent, some of them aged men who would never wear any clothes but those of little girls, and some of them blear-eyed women who had grown to weigh as much as twenty stone through lack of exercise, or even of daylight. It was less expensive than sending them to an institution.

Pat Geraghty showed up well in comparison with these, since he only suffered from delusions of grandeur. He believed that nobody but himself could do things properly. The confusing feature about this belief was that he was more or less right. He was a good workman, who took pains about his work in the style of an English laborer. If there were a pigsty to be floored with concrete, he cleaned out the excrements and even the mud until he got to a hard foundation, before he started. Almost everybody else within ten miles of Burkestown chucked the concrete on top of the litter and let it crack.

His delusions of grandeur were therefore backed by an amount of fact. Unfortunately he had the further disability of being unable to leave the work of other people alone. However good or bad it was, he pulled it to bits and did it again himself. This had a discouraging, even an exasperating, effect upon his mates. A workman who had spent the whole day building a clamp for mangolds hardly felt pleased to see it dashed to the earth by Pat's demonic energy, even if the latter were going to rebuild it. Also, of course, everything took twice as long to do, since it had to be done twice. Consequently, all the laborers who worked with Pat ended by having a fight with him. He not only destroyed the work of other people, but also criticized it bitterly while in progress. Gangs of infuriated haymakers or harvesters used to drag him into some ditch or other and half beat the life out of him, but he still went on telling them what they were doing wrong.

After several of these assaults, Pat had taken to working by himself if possible. He had a certain amount of insight into his condition—knew at any rate that he could not "get on" with other workmen—and for some years he had earned a solitary living by ditching. Walking across the landscape of Cashelmor, which was like a flatter Buckinghamshire with fewer woods and an occasional small bog thrown in at intervals, the traveler would come upon a gash in the earth, and "Master" Geraghty slashing away at the bottom of it with the energy of twenty moles. If Pat knew the traveler, and particularly if he liked him, the latter would be detained for twenty minutes or more, to admire the ditch. No flattery could satisfy him. The beauty of the ditch, the smoothness, the workmanship, the enormous amount accomplished since morning, all had to be praised twice or three times, and then the Master was not satisfied.

He was only called the "Master" behind his back. He was unmarried, and lived with a sister who was deaf and dumb.

Mr. White had got mixed up with him by mistake. The man had been employed to clean out some ditches at Burkestown, and the deaf and dumb sister had, or had not, stolen two and a half pairs of stockings from the clothesline, or was suspected of having done so, and there was a metal wedge in it (for felling trees), and some additional complications about a stepfather and a workhouse and a Dutch barn, together with other details too complicated for narration at less than epic length. The upshot was that Pat Geraghty was about to be discharged—there had even been some talk about putting the Civic Guards on him, or it may have been on the sister—while Mr. White, wrongly, believed him, or them, to be innocent. Before he knew where he was, therefore, he had found himself to be the full-time employer of Geraghty, who was of no earthly use to him.

The second man, Tommy Plunkett, was a young fellow of twenty-three, with no particular characteristics. He was later taken up for infanticide, and severely cautioned not to do it again, but almost anybody could have been had for that. He was mechanically ignorant, though not so ignorant as Mikey, and any work that was done on the farm was done by him.

Philomena was remarkable for her family. She had twenty-three brothers and sisters, who all lived in the middle of a small bog with their parents, in a house about ten feet square. Her sisters were almost always with child, and one of them was said to have strangled her first-born because it was illegitimate, and buried it in the proper graveyard in a cardboard boot box. But as she had grown bored with digging and only covered the box with an inch of clay, it was dug up later by one of the starving dogs of the neighborhood. This created a good deal of indignation locally, and the *Cashelmor Independent* came out with the angry headline: DISGRACEFUL BEHAVIOR OF DOG.

Her bottom was black because she wiped her hands on it. Both she and Mrs. O'Callaghan were of opinion that fingers had been made before tools. They did everything with their fingers, from stirring the tea to mixing the black lead for the grates. When what they were mixing was edible, such as the mash for the turkeys, they licked them afterward and wiped them on their skirts behind. When it was not edible, they wiped them straightaway. The cumulative effect was much the same as that of the process used by medievalists in taking rubbings from brass tombs, and both Mrs. O'Callaghan and Philomena, when seen from a distance, offered well-stenciled negative views of their posteriors which were pleasing as well as odd. It was not that they always wiped their hands there. About half the time they did not wipe them at all, but used the nearest door handle.

Philomena's other peculiarity, if it could be called

a peculiarity round Burkestown, was that she was
providing for her twenty-three brothers and sisters by stealing Mr. White's wardrobe, which she
took home on Sunday afternoons under her blouse,
one piece at a time. She also had a fetishistic
leaning toward pencils and clean paper. Perhaps
she was going to write a book about the noble
simplicity of Irish life.

These three people were not present at the
Announcement, in Philomena's case because it happened to be her night off and she was taking
home one of Mr. White's shirts; in the case of the
others, because the visitation took place in the
evening, and they had gone to tea.

To put it briefly, the Archangel's message was
that there was going to be a second Flood, and
that the people at Burkestown were to build an
Ark. The reason for this did not come through
the Biblical language clearly, but there was a good
deal about President Truman, the daughters of
Noah, Mr. Attlee, gopher wood, the Abomination
of Desolation, atomic bombs, etc.

Now it may seem easy to build an Ark, to anybody who has not done so, but there were difficul-
ties connected with such an enterprise, which were
sufficient to keep Mr. White awake until four
o'clock next morning: at first, while he discussed
the visitation with the O'Callaghans in all its aspects, and afterward, in bed, while he tried to
figure out the problem of construction.

Before we deal with this, however, it seems necessary to make a few remarks about our hero's
character. He was a childish man, in spite of his
amoebae, and he was confiding, and he nearly
always told the truth. This was out of laziness, as
he had found that it was easier to be truthful and
swindled, instead of going to the trouble of making up lies in order to swindle other people. Some-

times he grew ashamed of this laziness, about once a year, and tried to tell a few hard-working lies; but he told them so badly, with such a shifty look in his eye, that nobody believed them for a moment. This discouraged him. Fortunately, however, it did not matter how much he told the truth round Burkestown, because nobody in that locality ever told it, and consequently nobody believed it. Indeed, Mr. White's truthfulness had the curious effect of making the aborigines consider that he was the most cunning liar they had ever met. Unaccustomed to hearing the truth in any form, they were baffled by his veracity, and came to fear him greatly in a bargain. For instance, if he were selling one of the pigs which he kept on the refuse of the garden, he might say to the buyer: "I am afraid that this pig is not so fat as he should be. You see, if you put your hand here between the shoulder blades, you can feel the backbone." Far from lowering the price of the thin pig, this often had the effect of putting a couple of guineas on it: for the buyer immediately concluded that Mr. White had some intensely subtle reason for not selling, and became half mad to secure the prize.

Another feature of his character was that he was generally pursuing some theory or other, often dealing with archaeology or biology or history. For instance, he had a theory about warfare. He said that there were some 275,000 separate species in the animal kingdom, but that out of this huge number there were only a dozen or so which indulged in true war, i.e., which would band together in order to attack bands of their own species. The guilty dozen included H. sapiens, one termite, several ants, and possibly, though Mr. White was unsure of this, the domestic bee. If, said he, only twelve or so out of 275,000 will go to war, then obviously we can discover the true cause of warfare by looking for some Highest Common Factor which is found among the twelve, but not found among the 274,988 others. Eventually he had discovered that the H.C.F. was not Property nor several of the other things which had been suggested, but the making of a *territorial claim*. All twelve made a claim to territory other than the nest itself, and he could discover no pacific species which made such a claim. Also the few varieties of H. sapiens which did not make a territorial claim— the Lapps, Eskimos, and other true nomads— remained at peace. Mr. White said that the only thing necessary to abolish warfare was to abolish territory, i.e., to do away with artificial boundaries, nationalism, tariffs, and so on.

In the course of his researches into the behavior of belligerent ants, he naturally had to experiment. He had invented a test for finding out whether a given species of ant made a territorial claim in the natural state—for he considered that experiment in captivity was misleading—and it was this: He would take a colony of the ant in question, carry it a mile or so in order to cut out the chance of relationship, and he would try to establish it as close as possible to another nest of the same species. By seeing how close the new colony was tolerated, on various radii from the established nest, he was able to plot a rough map of the territory claimed by that nest.

Now this was all very well with *L. flavus* or with what he still insisted on calling *M. rubra*, for they were readily accessible on the farm. But when he needed to interfere with *F. fusca*, he had to go to the bog. There, as he crouched with gusty beard in a tweed hat turned down all round, which made him look like the Emperor of Abyssinia, and pored upon the maneuvers of some agitated ant with a spot of white paint on its bottom, a hundred pairs of prehistoric Celtic eyes observed him craftily, from their concealment behind turf stacks, walls, donkeys, and so on. What was he doing? The only things they ever did themselves were either wicked or cunning, so they naturally concluded that Mr. White was doing the same. Either he was a German spy signaling to the English, or he was an English spy signaling to the Germans, or he was a sorcerer making a spell, or he was burying his money, or he was digging up somebody else's money; but at all events he was overreaching somebody, as they would have wished to do themselves. The moment he left the bog, dozens of semianthropoid figures would shamble or scuttle across to the place where he had last squatted, and there, fighting and bickering for precedence, they would commence to search, dig, scratch, or throw about the stones with feverish energy.

One of his experiments had entailed the use of colored water in a bottle. He colored the water with red ink. The fact was that most ants objected to daylight, but, as they saw a different spectrum from Mr. White's, they had little objection to red light. When he wanted to watch what was going on in a colony, without disturbing the ants, he would cover it with a bottle of diluted red ink, because he could look in by this means while the ants still considered that they were unobserved. Naturally the bottle had to be left *in situ* from day to day, a kind of red skylight into the nest, because to move it would have been a cause of disturbance. To protect the bottle from stray bullocks, Mr. White used to cover it with a stone when he went home for tea.

The bottles of red ink, invariably stolen as soon as he had gone away, were a source of wonder round Burkestown. Some put them up the chimney and waited for them to turn into crocks of gold; some strewed their contents over a neighbor's boundary to induce ill luck; some gave them to their cattle as a specific against contagious abortion; and some drank them themselves, as a cure for rheumatism, hemorrhoids, or the itch. Eventually, since he could never complete an experiment, he had grown so tired of having his bottles stolen that he had gone to the chemist and bought some tartar emetic, putting a good dose in each bottle that he left. Alas, this only had an opposite effect. It made his unwanted patients so violently sick that they, impressed by the magnitude of their vomits, testified all the more vehemently to the potency of the charm. His reputation as a magician had increased by leaps and bounds, so that it had become even more impossible to leave the ink bottles anywhere.

Well then, it can be seen that he was the very person to build an Ark.

But he lay awake for all that, until four o'clock in the morning, trying to solve a series of problems which presented themselves in connection with the enterprise.

In the first place, he had a slight mental adjustment to make on the subject of God. If there really were Archangels, there presumably must also exist the Hierarchy of Heaven, and the amoebae must have made a mistake. It is a surprising fact that he was able to adjust his ideas to the new basis with scarcely any alteration.

Secondly, there was the question of materials. To build a wooden Ark according to the Biblical pattern, and one, moreover, which would be large enough to accommodate numerous pairs of animals, would cost him several thousand pounds. He only had six hundred in the bank. Also, however much he tried to believe in it, he could not convince himself that the Biblical Ark would have floated—and particularly not in the Irish Sea, where, he supposed, their Flood would eventually lead them. Apart from the prohibitive cost of buying timber and employing labor and erecting scaffolding, he only had a vague idea of the technique necessary for putting a curve on the bottom boards.

He solved all this with a characteristic flash of inspiration, by deciding to turn the haybarn upside down, and to use that.

The third problem was a scruple of conscience. It was evident that he would never be able to build the Ark by himself, though he might be able to do so with the assistance of Pat Geraghty. On the other hand, the Archangel had said nothing about taking Pat Geraghty with them. It seemed, to say the least of it, unfair to employ the unfortunate man in building it, and then, when the Flood came, to leave him drowning, refusing him asylum in the very structure which he had helped to rear. Mr. White solved this by deciding (a) that the Almighty must obviously take a reasonable view of the problems involved and, being omniscient, would probably have His own solution in view already, (b) perhaps He would arrange for Pat Geraghty to refuse to come in the Ark of his own accord, or dispose of him in some other way, (c) in any case, he was paying Geraghty 36/- a week, and (d) it might be possible to find him a wife, so as to include them both as cargo, with the other pairs of animals.

When he had got so far as this, the real difficulty began to stick out. If a person had seen an Archangel and received Its instructions, it was natural enough to build an Ark when told to do so. But the neighbors had not seen it; nor had Pat Geraghty. It was only reasonable that everybody should consider the whole thing to be insane, and it was possible that Geraghty would refuse to help. Even if he did not refuse, and even if the reaction of the neighbors were to be left to look after itself, how was Mr. White to break the news? He somehow did not like the idea of telling Geraghty that the Archangel Michael had come down the chimney.

Perhaps, he thought, it would be best not to tell him that it is an Ark at all. I might say that it was going to be a swimming bath, for instance, and trust to the proverbial madness of Englishmen to make it sound credible. Obviously I shall have to tell him that it is going to be something, or he will not be able to understand his work.

The worst of it was that the hay was already in big cocks, in the fields, and would need to be drawn to the hay barn at any moment.

CHAPTER
IV

Mr. White got up next morning an hour earlier than usual. That is, he got up at half past nine, which was the hour at which Mrs. O'Callaghan lit the kitchen fire when Philomena was at home, and Mikey went to pretend to milk. (When feeling bored or tired, Mikey used to leave the cows unmilked, however, and, as he seldom troubled to feed them in the winter, they generally lost about four of them each year.)

He made his way to the garden, where he found Pat Geraghty unearthing a row of celery, which he had earthed up himself the day before.

"Well, Pat."

"Well, sorr."

"I see you are taking the clay off my celery."

"Ye had it earthed wid the dirt atween the stems."

"I see. Well, I suppose you will be earthing it up again when you have finished?"

"Sure, I will. Ye can trust me for that, sorr. I'll have it earthed up in a minute, the way you won't see another row of celery like it in the County Kildare."

"Good. Well now, h'm."

He turned away, conscious that his eyes were still puffy from sleep and that he had not yet made up his mind about the swimming bath. He picked a late pea pod, for something to do while he considered, and began to eat the peas. It always took two hours in the morning, before his head began to spin.

When he had eaten the peas without enlightenment, he fell back on his usual inefficiency and told the truth.

"I suppose you could not believe it, if I told you that the Archangel Michael had come to Burkestown last night?"

Pat Geraghty took this as a reflection on his powers of belief. He said with some hostility: "I could believe it, then."

"You could not believe that It told us to build an Ark?" asked Mr. White incredulously.

"I could believe that, and a great dale more."

The bloodless victory made him feel dizzy. He blew his nose hard, to promote thought, and looked at Pat to see if he were in earnest, which he was. Obviously he would have to be carefully managed, if the fruits of victory were not to be thrown away.

"You must have a wonderful faculty of belief," he said flatteringly.

Pat leaned on his shovel and acknowledged the compliment grandly.

"We have to build an Ark because there is to be a second Flood. I thought you might be able to help—but then I thought it would be too difficult for you."

"Is it me build an Ark? I could build that, and more to it."

"We were going to turn the hay barn upside down, and use that. But the girders are heavy. I said that I did not think you would be able for the work."

"I could turn that barn over in three minutes.

"And," added Pat, beginning to fire with enthusiasm, "a grand Ark she would make for any man."

"We shall have to bolt a keel on it, or it will roll over."

This was a false step.

"A keel, is it? That barn doesn't need a keel. I'll make an Ark out of that barn that ye wouldn't knock a roll out of her in the Romantic Ocean."

Without a keel, as even Mr. White could see, the trough-shaped roof of a galvanized Dutch barn had no chance—and it had never yet been possible to make Pat Geraghty change his mind. Fortunately his own mind had begun to spin under the stimulus of crisis, and he was able to stage a comeback.

"At any rate, you would not be able to bolt a girder or a piece of four-by-two along the ridge?"

"I could bolt that asy. It's what I will do, sorr, to prevent her rolling."

"Let's go and look at it, then."

On their way out of the garden, they found Brownie turning somersaults on the asparagus bed, which provoked a faint wail from her master.

"Oh, darling, must you?"

"Sure, she won't do it any harm. It doesn't be any use, anyway."

Pat's horizon was bounded by spuds, cabbage, bacon, and oatmeal, and, as the other's imagination rioted in such things as melons, celeriac, kohlrabi, Indian corn, endive, salsify, and so forth, there was a coolness between them on horticultural subjects. Pat stroked her, as a reward for her iconoclasm, and Mr. White stroked her too, for fear of having offended her by complaining.

The hay barn was like this:

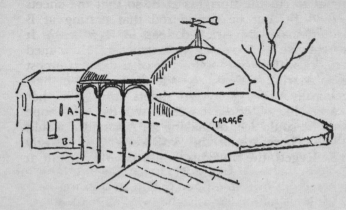

It was fairly new and quite sound—they were still paying installments on it—and it had a blue enamel plaque on one end, which said:

The east end of it had a corrugated iron garage leaning against it, and, on the roof of the barn at that end, there was the tripod of the Wincharger, which would have to be taken down. At the west end there was a passage leading to the cowsheds and the horse stable, with the oats loft above.

The hay barn was about eighteen feet high, forty-eight feet long, and twenty-four feet wide.

"We shall have to saw through the uprights there . . ."

Mr. White pointed to the line marked A on the picture, but kept a discreet silence about the length of the corrugated sheets, which came down to the line marked B. It would have been more convenient to cut the uprights at B, so that the sheets would fit, but he considered that cutting at B would make the Ark too deep for her beam. It would give her too much superstructure. He wanted an Ark with only a foot or two of seaboard, almost a submarine, for he hoped to deck her over hermetically with corrugated sheets, and to let her wallow like a corked bottle. It was the only hope that he could see, of making an Ark which would float. Therefore, if the Ark were to lie mostly submerged, the uprights would have to be cut at A, and this would mean that the sheeting on the ends and sides would also have to be shortened. It would have to be done by cutting perforations, like dotted lines, with the hammer and cold chisel, and then by breaking off the unnecessary end by bending at the line. There were thirty-four sheets to cut, which would be a nuisance, and this was why Mr. White hurried Geraghty past that particular part of the program, before he could fully understand it and begin to contradict.

"Are the uprights too strong to cut with the hack saw? We have twelve spare blades."

The form of the question, which was neither a *num* nor a *nonne*, left Pat free to give an unbiased answer. His questioner was not sure whether the hack would stand up to the girders, and wanted an opinion.

"They don't be so thick as they look."

The uprights were in girder form: that is, a section through them would have been in the shape of a capital H. It was decided that the little hack saw would manage.

"How shall we get it down?"

One of Geraghty's accomplishments was moving felled trees—he could manage them up to a ton or more—and Mr. White did have a faint hope that he would be able to invent some wonderful lever-age, to lift the roof off in one piece. However, Pat gave the sensible reply.

"We shall have to take her to bits, sorr, and put her together on the ground."

"How long do you think it will take?"

"We could do it in two weeks. All thim bolts will be rusted."

"We shall have to caulk the seams . . ."

Mr. White corrected himself quickly: "I suppose you won't be able to think of a way to keep the water from trickling between the sheets?"

"Why wouldn't I think? I mane to fill those joins wid stuffing, sorr, and ye'll see her ride like a duck."

"What sort of stuffing?"

But this was too fast for a person who had only just been faced with the problem. He himself, during the night, had considered the merits of putty—which would be too rigid and would not take to the metal—of moss—but he was not an authority on moss—and of torn rags well ham-mered in, where necessary, with tar on them. The last had seemed the most suitable.

"It would be no good," said Mr. White craftily, "stuffing the seams with rags and tar."

"And why not, sorr, if ye plaze? It's what I was going to tell ye this minute, only for you spaking so fast on one thing after another.

"Rags," continued Geraghty, in a hectoring tone, "is the only yoke for jobs like thim. No Ark would float widout thim. Ye don't understand these things, sorr, begging your pardon, being a gintleman, but lave you all to me, and it won't be far asthray."

"I see. Yes. Then we will use tarred rags as you suggest. Now do you know anybody who would lend us a long ladder? At least, that is, I suppose it is no good using a ladder?"

"Sure we must use a ladder. How would we get up widout it?"

"No, of course not. Well, then. You could not get the loan of a ladder, could you?"

"I could get the loan of anything."

"I am sure you could. Ahem. Yes. This ladder you were speaking about . . ."

"Our ladder does be too short."

"I know it is. No, I mean, now that you mention it, I realize that it is too short. Is there any other ladder that you happen to know of, which would not be too short?"

"Our ladder would not be too short if we tied her on the dray, sorr. That's where I have ye."

"It won't reach the roof."

"Sure, ye can jump on that roof from the top of the garridge."

"I daresay you can, Pat; but I can't."

"We'll put a chair on the garridge, sorr, or a table and chair, and ye'll be up in a minute."

"I am not going to stand on a chair on a table on a sloping corrugated roof.

"Once," continued Mr. White, warming at the reminiscence, "I put a ladder on top of a table, when I wanted to paint the outside of an upstairs window. The table turned over when I was at the top, with a paint pot, and do you know, Pat, as I fell—I can still see the stones of the wall streaming past my nose—I screeched out *to myself*, 'Look out!' "

"You had no sinse," explained Pat.

"No."

"We'll tie the chair and table with a reins."

"Well, if you can make it firm, I suppose it will have to do."

"Is it me can make it firm, sorr? There's no . . ."

"Yes, yes. I know you can. I know there is not. Now the question is, are the nuts on the bolts outside the roof or inside it?"

They stood craning up into the middle distance, trying to see the details of construction. The great gray trough spanned dimly over them with its regular fluting, which, like an optical delusion, harried the eye for some reason and made it difficult to focus.

"The ties of the girders is bolted inside, and the sheets is bolted outside."

"The bolts are galvanized. They ought not to be rusty. And look here, Pat, there are diamond-shaped galvanized washers on the bolts outside. And each flute of a sheet fits into the end flute of the next sheet, so that it is practically airtight. We shall not need much caulking. I must say it is a lovely job, when you come to look into it."

"That's not a lovely job, sorr. That's a scamped job. I could have done that job so that there would not be another job like it in the County Kildare."

"You will be able to prove it with the Ark, Pat. There must not be another Ark like it in the . . ."

"And nor there will be, Mr. White."

Pat solemnly raised his fist in the air, took off his felt hat, and said: "My Ark will be an Ark which they'll come from London to see the like of it."

"I hope not."

The yellow eye, swiveling in search of insult, made him explain as quickly as possible.

"They might try to stop us, Pat. They might think we were mad. I mean, they might not have your faculty of belief. Listen, Pat, don't tell anybody what we are building. Let them find out."

"I take your meaning, sorr."

"And, sorr"—the hat came off again—"wid the help of God, we'll bate them yet."

"Amen."

They shook hands in their emotion, and the project was concluded.

CHAPTER
V

In the dairy, Mikey and Mrs. O'Callaghan were poring over the lid of the churn. It was a tumbling churn, which they had used for the past twenty-three years, but seldom without a struggle with the lid. They seemed to have forgotten about the Archangel Michael, Ark and all.

Mrs. O'Callaghan said gaily: "You'll have to put your hand over it, Mr. White. It needs your head."

In ordinary circumstances this would have made him feel cross. Mrs. O'Callaghan's reaction to the general incapacity at Burkestown was run on the following lines: (1) if I cannot screw up a screw, it is because I have no head, (2) if Mr. White can screw up a screw, it is because he has a head, (3) having a head or not is a gift of God, (4) since the matter rests entirely on God's caprice, I have nothing to reproach myself with, for not having a head and for not being able to screw up a screw, (5) therefore I need not trouble to learn how to screw up a screw.

Mr. White was fond of Mrs. O'Callaghan, a weakness which commonly makes people anxious to improve one another. This made him feel angry when she referred to his head—because he knew that she was using it as an excuse for her own laziness. He believed in striving and thriving, faring ever there as here. It made him impatient of

45

the fatalism which prevailed around him, and this caused him, in his relations with the Irish, to resemble the White Rabbit in *Alice in Wonderland*. Do you remember, when Alice got herself stuck in the rabbit's house through growing too big, and had to thrust her arm out of the window, and frightened the rabbit himself into a cucumber frame by making a grab at him?

Next came an angry voice—the Rabbit's— "Pat! Pat! Where are you?" And then a voice she had never heard before, "Sure then I'm here! Digging for apples, yer honour!"

"Digging for apples, indeed!" said the Rabbit angrily. "Here, come and help me out of *this*!" (Sounds of more broken glass.)

"Now tell me, Pat, what's that in the window?"

"Sure, it's an arm, yer honour!" (He pronounced it "arrum.")

"An arm, you goose! Who ever saw one that size? Why, it fills the whole window!"

"Sure it does, yer honour: but it's an arm for all that."

"Well it's got no business there, at any rate: go and take it away!"

On this occasion, however, Mr. White was in excellent humor over the Ark, and did not wish to command anything to be taken away. He examined the churn and found that the thread was worn on one of the screws which clamped the lid. An ordinary bolt, from his tool cupboard, would act as a substitute.

He went to the playroom for the bolt.

The male swallow had managed to wedge himself, as usual, between the panes of glass in the open sash window. Mr. White rescued him, threw him out of the window, and caught a horsefly which was sitting on one of the panes. It was a fly which the swallow had himself brought, before his accident. He went over to the nest, which prevented the tool cupboard from shutting, and awarded the fly. Then he forgot about the bolt and fell into a brown study opposite the cupboard, summing up his tools. When one comes to think of it, he resembled not only the White Rabbit, but also the White Knight. He had the latter's interest in practical constructions.

He was proposing to build an Ark which would float, presumably for forty days, and possibly in stormy weather.

He had: the homemade lathe, which wobbled; two handsaws and a hack saw with twelve blades; an ordinary plane; two plow planes and a fourth plane with a blade shaped like the letter U; two common screwdrivers and a spring screwdriver; two chisels and a marl; a clawed hammer; a pair of metal shears; a brace and various bits for it, but unfortunately it was not a ratchet brace; six files; a wood rasp; a thing for cutting the angles on picture frames; a paraffin blowlamp and soldering outfit; a square and a T square and some geometrical instruments; a spirit level; two putty knives and a trowel; a diamond; a pair of wire cutters; two carborundum stones; and plenty of emery or sandpaper. He also had a good store of materials such as nails, screws, hinges, locks, bolts, brackets, copper rivets, studs, and so on. In the garage there was a certain amount of wood, mainly planks, two-by-two, four-by-two, three-by-three, slats, and the prepared wood for holding window glass—also some sheets of glass left over from the greenhouse, and a little three-ply. There were two cross-cut saws. Finally there were the tools of his motor car, which included pliers, wrenches, spanners, and the rest of the usual outfit; and there were the farm tools—crowbar, cold chisel, ax, wedges, and so on.

He said to Brownie: "We shall need some ropes to lower the girders. It won't be safe to let them drop."

The floor of the barn was cobbled, like the rest of the yard.

In the end, he collected the bolt and went down to the churn.

Mikey and Mrs. O'Callaghan were both red, and had begun to sweat a bit. As he came in at the door, he heard Mrs. O'Callaghan saying: "Well, it's not me fault, I forgot it."

The attribution of faults had become so automatic that they would sometimes prove it was not their fault by proving it was. Mikey would say: "Why can't I have me tea in a pot?", and Mrs. O'Callaghan would reply: "Well, it's not me fault, I broke it."

He fixed the churn.

He said: "What about animals?"

"Animals?"

"For the Ark."

"Sure, we don't want animals?"

"What else is the Ark for?"

"Oh, Lor," said Mikey. "Shall we have a tiger?"

"And one of them things with ears?"

"What do you mean, things with ears?"

"Like a bull, but ten times bigger, and it swims under the water, and clings to stones."

"Do you mean an elephant?"

"Yes," said Mrs. O'Callaghan, "an elephant. It has red stripes, and hair all over."

"But an elephant . . ."

"Perhaps it's what I mean a mousekeeter. It be's as big as a house."

"Well . . ."

"But if we have a tiger," said Mikey, who knew

how to stick to essentials where danger was concerned, "it will have us ate up."

"So far as I can see," said Mr. White, "it would be unreasonable to expect us to take any animals except the ones we can get ourselves. If the Archangel Michael had wanted a zoo, It should have gone to Mr. Flood in Dublin. It did not do so. It came to us. I therefore assume that we were the right people to come to—that we were the kind of people who would provide the kind of thing that was wanted. Perhaps the next world, after the deluge, is to be colonized by domestic animals. It would be interesting to see what happened. In any case, I don't think we need take anything that we cannot get hold of locally. For one thing, there would not be room. Evidently no Ark can hope to contain two each of 275,000 species, even if we persuaded the fish to swim behind. Besides, look at the food we should need to take. No, my idea is that we need only carry what we can get round Burkestown, and I shall stick to that until we hear to the contrary."

"Then we don't need a tiger?"

"No."

"Thank God."

"And Mr. White," added Mrs. O'Callaghan automatically. He had once complained that she was always thanking God for things which he did for her himself, so that, since then, she had fallen into the habit of making this addition.

"Must we take the bull?"

"I'm afraid so, Mikey."

"Suppose he goes loose."

"We shall have to fix him so that he can't. And look here, we shall have to take two of everything, but I think we ought to see to it that the female is with young already. As a matter of fact—wait a bit—I think we can do without the bull after all. It will be sufficient to take an adult female of each species and a juvenile male. This will save space. Instead of taking a huge great bull, we can take a small entire bull calf. Only the females need to be full-grown, and those so as to give us the additional margin of insurance which they offer by being already gravid. We must see to it that the young they are carrying have a different paternity from the male which goes with them. This will be a help against inbreeding. Now . . ."

"Shall we have to take the bees?"

"I will deck the Ark over, Mikey, and we can bolt some lengths of two-by-two along the deck. Then we can screw a hive to these and keep anything else that is dangerous or not important up above. If they wash overboard, it can't be helped. Anyway, we shall have to save space."

"Thim bees . . ."

"They won't sting you. And, by the way, we shall have to take care what animals we choose. What a difficult job it is, when one comes to think of it! The balance of Nature. It makes one feel like a god. You see, if we take rabbits they might multiply too fast and eat up the corn we grow—we must take all the oats, wheat, and barley we can stow—and so we should have to take foxes, to keep down the rabbits, but the foxes might steal the lambs, and so on. It's very difficult indeed. If we don't take various small insect-eating birds, there may come a plague of bugs to eat up our fruit crop—we must take the seeds of everything we can think of—and if we do take small birds, we shall have to take hawks to keep them down, or they will eat the fruit themselves. As for bees, unless we take them, there will be nothing to pollinate the vegetables, and we shall have to live on nuts and cereals. Yes, by Jove, and there's the question of worms. I won't take two earthworms—

anyway, they are hermaphroditic. I will take a whole box of them, with earth. Do you know, Mrs. O'Callaghan, there are fifty-three thousand worms in every garden acre and they turn over the soil to a depth of seven inches in thirty years? If the worms were not turning over the soil for us all the time, the earth would get a sterile skin, like earthenware, and nothing would grow on it. Consequently there would be no vegetables and therefore no animals which feed on vegetables or on each other. In fact, if there were no worms in the world, there would be no life at all, except in the sea. We must take a great many worms. They will all have been drowned. Worms are much more important than human beings, as I told you in my booklet."

"But, Mr. White," said Mrs. O'Callaghan faintly, "we know that God made Man in His own image."

"I see. Well now, there's the question of trying to balance our future Nature. In my opinion, it is hopeless to try. It is far too difficult."

"Mr. White will be able for it, never fear."

"No, I won't be able. No single person could ever know enough. It is too complicated. All I can suggest is that we should take two of everything we can lay our hands on, and leave the rest to the Archangel Michael.

"I can't help thinking," he added diffidently, "that we could do without the green fly."

"And weeds," he cried, thumping the churn, "think of it, they will all be drowned!"

"Will Titsy be drowned?" asked Mrs. O'Callaghan.

Titsy was a black cat in which she put great faith, on account of its color. Mrs. O'Callaghan's various beliefs, apart from halos and angels, included fortunetellers, patent medicines, not meeting weasels or redheaded women or magpies on a journey, never lighting three cigarettes with one match, never having three candles in one room, killing cocks if they crowed at the wrong time, and, indeed, about seven thousand other superstitions, both religious and secular, which provided a continuum in which to lead her life. Mr. White disapproved of all seven thousand, including Titsy. He always tauntingly called Titsy "the holy cat," which exasperated Mrs. O'Callaghan, probably because it was true.

"Of course Titsy will be drowned. What do you think this Flood is? Everything will be drowned. Unless, of course, we take her with us."

"Will Mrs. James of Ecclestown be drowned?"

"Goodness me, don't you understand? Haven't we been talking about the Flood all night? Certainly Mrs. James will be drowned, and Father Byrne, and Dan Ryan, and Mrs. Ryan, and the whole bloody lot of them, and a good job too. Can't you understand it's a *Flood?*"

"Will the Bishop be drowned?"

"Oh, my God, yes! *Everybody* will be drowned."

"Shall we be drowned?" asked Mikey apprehensively.

Mr. White sat on the handle of the separator and ran his fingers through his hair.

"Look," he said. "When we have got the Ark built, it will begin to rain. Perhaps it will be snow or hail. Or perhaps there will be a general subsidence of the earth's crust. In fact, I suppose that's what there will be. After all, there is only a certain amount of water on the globe and you can't conjure more out of the sky, because the rain itself is sucked from the sea. So, if the waters are going to cover the face of the earth, I suppose it is the face of the earth which will have to sink. There may even be volcanic eruptions. Or the floor of the ocean might rise. . . . It will be something to do with atomic energy. . . .

"In any case," he continued desperately, "there will be water. *Water*. Do you understand? There will be water everywhere—water in Dublin, water in London, water in Cashelmor, water in the Arth and the Haggard and the Calf Park and the Tillage Field and the Lawn and the Slane Meadow and Back of Kelly's."

These were the names of some of the fields at Burkestown.

"Will there be water in the Racecourse?"

This was the name of a field on the farm next door.

"*Yes!* Good God, don't you understand English? There will be water *everywhere*. Do you understand that?"

"Yes," said Mrs. O'Callaghan doubtfully.

"Well then. When this water comes, you and I and Mikey and Brownie and the holy cat and all the animals will get into the hay barn, which will be upside down, and we shall float away on the water while the rest of the world is drowned.

"Come to think of it," added Mr. White, feeling doubtful in turn, "what will happen to the people in liners and battleships? Unless the Flood lasts so long that they starve, I don't see how they can very well be drowned. Perhaps it will be that they will have no seeds to plant, when they do land, and so they will starve afterward on the slime. However, we must leave all that to the Archangel Michael.

"Now, when we have floated away in the hay barn, the entire surface of the world will remain under water for an indefinite length of time, perhaps for forty days if we are to go by the last Flood—though that seems very little to starve a battleship—and when the water does go down at last, there will be nothing there but wet mud."

"It will have me carpets destroyed!"

"You won't find your carpets at all. For one thing, I don't suppose we shall come down again where we started. There will be currents in the ocean, presumably, even if the subsidence of the earth's crust alters their direction. We may find that we have been carried into the Arctic zone. By the way, we shall have to take warm clothes. We can always leave them off, if we strike a tropical climate, but we can't put them on unless we have them. Mrs. O'Callaghan, you must take your fur coat.

"And, so far as that goes, the general subsidence may alter the climate itself. . . . But I was telling you about the slime. Well then, this slime will have been under water for forty days or whatever the time is, and it will have been salt water. You must not think of it as if it were just a flood of the Slane. It will be a Flood of the main ocean mass on the whole globe, and presumably the salt water will swallow the fresh. I don't know, but I suppose that forty days under sea water will kill the trees and everything. That is why we shall have to take seeds. As soon as it has gone down, and the slime is firm enough, we shall have to set to work and plough and sow. By the way, we must take a plough, and I shall have to work it. Nancy will have to pull it by herself, or with the cow. The other horse will be a colt. And we shall have to take enough stores to keep us going for a whole year, until our first harvest."

"Will you take me rubber boots?" asked Mikey.

He and Mrs. O'Callaghan had come to regard the affair as Mr. White's.

"Yes, if you like. They will wear out, of course, and then we shall have to make pampooties. But really, it is no good talking about all this now. We shall have to write lists in the evenings. Let me see, I came in for a table and chair. . . ."

He captured one of the kitchen chairs and went out to find Geraghty, but came back again immediately, still carrying the chair.

"Mikey, you and Tommy Plunkett will have to go on with the harvest as usual. We shall need the grain to take with us. We will take some hayseed too. And, Mrs. O'Callaghan, where's Philomena?"

"She's doing the room."

"Send her home this evening. Give her the evening off. Give her a month's notice or something. And don't talk about the Flood in front of her."

Philomena was listening outside the door in her stockinged feet, but this was one of the aspects of life round Burkestown for which Mr. White always forgot to allow. It made no difference, however, as she had only understood one word in ten, and she told her twenty-three brothers and sisters that evening that the O'Callaghans were thinking of going to America.

He went out again with the chair.

He came back to say: "I'm afraid I shall have to take down the Wincharger. I will try to put it up again somewhere, for the time being. I might be able to make a casing for the drawing-room chimney, and bolt the tripod on that."

Soon, as Mrs. O'Callaghan peeped from a slit in the kitchen shutters, he could be seen with Pat Geraghty crawling and thundering and banging on the lovely gray arc of the hay barn. The sun was shining for once, and a deep blue sky was behind the columned gray. Ultramarine was the enamel plaque, orange the blade of the Wincharger —whose taut wire stays sliced the sky with mathematical definition. Mathematical, too, were the corrugated sheets with their marshaled shadows, and all looked clean and certain in the sunlight.

Mrs. O'Callaghan kept the shutters half closed, and worked in a submarine gloom which gave her rheumatism, because she said that if the sun shone on the kitchen range it would put the fire out.

CHAPTER
VI

It was evening. The three sat round a scrubbed table in the whitewashed kitchen, under the electric light.

Mr. White had insisted on making lists.

Mrs. O'Callaghan had a ruled copybook, a pen with a crossed nib, and an ink bottle with one millimeter of crust at the bottom. Mr. White had an enormous folio notebook or ledger, and a fountain pen with green ink. They had given Mikey a piece of brown paper and a six-H pencil, which was the only one that Philomena had left in the house. Mikey had broken the point off, but continued to write with the wood, with much the same effect.

Their lists were headed: ANIMALS.

Mr. White had decided that they would make different lists each night, pool them, and talk them over. One night it was to be Animals, the next night Tools, the third night Seeds, the fourth night Provisions, and so on. He was writing fast. Mrs. O'Callaghan was writing intermittently, in the round, laborious characters which she used for shopping lists. Mikey was writing like an artist. That is, he touched his word up now and then—he had written only one—by putting a dot, or another letter, or by changing an established letter for another one on top of it.

57

Brownie was sitting in a corner, eating the latest glue. She was an animal who suffered from crazes, like her master. They say that wise men grow to resemble the creatures they are interested in, and that Darwin ended by looking like an ape. This is true conversely, at any rate, for most animals grow to resemble the masters they are interested in, and Brownie was no exception. She had put up with so many snakes, falcons, goshawks, merlins, ravens, ants, goat moths, hedgehogs, and other assorted fauna collected by Mr. White that in the end she had taken to collecting herself. For instance, she was keen on week-old chickens. Every spring, when these came round, she attended all their meals. She also caught them in her mouth, without hurting them, and carried them into the dining room, where she liberated them under the table and watched them run. The hens, ever after, in adult life, fled upon the approach of Brownie. Another of her interests was the insect world. She spent a good deal of time catching flies, or taunting the bees in the hall. She was a student of wood-boring wasps, which she would watch on the workshop window sill all day long. She had been the proud owner of a wild baby rabbit, which she used to take to bed with her, in her master's bed, and also of a young leveret. Neither of these had been much pleased at having to sleep with Brownie and Mr. White, and the rabbit particularly had often flown into a passion at the general perversity of the situation, and had bitten them both. People seem to think that wild rabbits are charming little balls of fluff, but they are really very choleric animals, with no tolerance at all. Other pets kept by Brownie included ducks, turkeys, and an orphan lamb. She was interested in the swallows on the tool cupboard, and devoted to hedgehogs, for which she had a special bark. She did not like puppies.

The craze for Nature Study, however, was not the only one she had. Mr. White possessed varied interests, and so did she. There was carpentry, for instance, which was perhaps the latest of his digressions. Poor Brownie could hardly saw or hammer, but at least she collected the spare pieces of wood, and kept them under the dining-room table. So far as gardening was concerned, she collected most of the root crops and tubers, which she also stored under the table. She had, besides, a rubber ball.

Her master was a second-rate writer, and that was the way in which he earned such living as he had. It was the only occupation she was unable to share. When he sat at the typewriter, Brownie sat beside him and groaned continuously—perhaps she was doing her best to imitate the machine. When he wrote with a pencil, in an armchair, she sat on his lap and sighed, in order to be in it as much as possible.

The glue must have been due to the Ark. It was used in construction. Mr. White had been trying to boil it in a soup tin, because he had no gluepot, and she had discovered it, in the solid state, at the bottom. This was what she was eating. Being at the bottom, it was almost out of reach of her tongue. However, she had bitten dents in the tin all round, and she could reach some of the glue, and it made her froth at the mouth.

It is only fair to add that she was good at her own profession. She was the rarest of all creatures, a steady retrieving setter. Everybody had told Mr. White that it was quite impossible to train a setter to retrieve without losing steadiness, which had been sufficient to make him determined to do so, and he had done so; except, of course, that it is really the dog who trains her master, not vice versa.

Mr. White had spent a busy day. The Wincharger was dismantled, and there was part of the casing already bolted round the drawing-room chimney. It had four holdfasts. There was enough charge in the batteries to give them light for a hundred hours on one twelve-watt bulb.

His list said:

Nancy and colt, not by her,
Friesian cow and bull calf ditto.
Nellie and male piglet ditto,
Sitting turkey and clutch,
Ditto hen,
Ditto duck,
Ewe and hogget, mountainy,
Diamond and Tiny (the farm dogs),
Brownie,
Titsy, I suppose,
Item, we ought to take a dove. I think it must really have been a homing pigeon, or else it would have sat down on the branch instead of carrying it home. It will need a mate or eggs.
Are rats really necessary?
Mouse ditto.
What about fleas?
Are lice any use?
Bats . . .

But it would be tedious to give the list at full length. It ran to fifteen folio pages, and included such rarities as ladybirds—to eat the green fly; dragon flies—to eat scale insects; gulls—to eat the daddy longlegs; shrew mice—to eat slugs; and stoats—to keep down the rabbits. If asked where the pests were coming from, Mr. White would have said that he was taking no chances with stow-aways. He would have added that he would probably take them himself, to keep down something else.

Mrs. O'Callaghan's list said:

Mr. White
Miky
Titssy
Browny
Nancy
Nely
Magy
Dimon
Tinny
The Bisshop

Except for the first two and the last, these were the names of various cows and other animals on the farm. Mr. White firmly crossed off the bishop.

Mikey's list said simply:

TABAKKEIGHE

"I suppose you think tobacco is an animal?"

Mikey looked guilty but obstinate. He liked it.

"How much do you smoke a week?"

"Four ounces."

"Then we should have to take a couple of hundredweight or more, to keep you going for the next twenty years. Do you know how much that would cost?"

"It would cost a pound or two."

"It would cost," said Mr. White, feverishly multiplying 240 by 16 on the margin of his list, "exactly one hundred and ninety-two pounds at one shilling an ounce, and you can't get it for that."

"Oh, Lor!"

"And yet—wait a moment—we do not know

what kind of climate we shall come down in. It might be suitable for growing tobacco. Remind me to take a lot of tropical seeds, when we begin the next list."

Mrs. O'Callaghan said earnestly: "What does this Flood be for?"

"For?"

"Well, why is it?"

"I suppose God must have got fed up with the human race—or the parts of the animal kingdom which we shall forget to take. He wants to start again with a clean slate, I suppose."

"It doesn't be much use starting wid us."

Now this was a point which our hero had been trying not to face on the roof during the day. Mr. and Mrs. O'Callaghan were childless, and past the work.

He said firmly: "Perhaps the Archangel Michael does not want to continue the human race. Perhaps It is purposely sending us because It does not want more humans. We would be needed to build the Ark and to navigate it and to look after the animals at first, but after that we may be intended to die out."

"You ought to get married, Mr. White."

"If the Archangel Michael wanted a married man, why didn't It choose one?"

"Think of all the little babies," said Mrs. O'Callaghan.

He thought of them. After the swallows and other animals, he would not have minded. It was the wife that had him terrified.

CHAPTER
VII

The Wincharger was transferred to a casing on the drawing-room chimney, where the jackdaws prevented fires from being lit.

In the drawing room there were: a beautiful piano, so far as the wood was concerned, but it had not been tuned for twenty-three years and the walls of Burkestown were made of a sweating stone which transmitted the climate freely; a stuffed badger in a case; two stuffed pheasants and a curlew on the piano, in a bower of dusty pampas grass arranged in pink glass pots; a whatnot with three black velvet cats on it and some dozens of china knickknacks; nine photographs, mainly of departed priests, in frames made of sea shells *(chenopus pes-pelicanus);* a piece of needlework like a sampler, dated 1889, with a black border, in memory of a departed bishop; a gramophone with a scarlet tin horn and fourteen records, including "Phil the Fluter's Ball" and "Angelus" sung by Clara Butt; a sofa and two armchairs; a Berlin-work fire screen, wonderfully well done by an auntie of Mikey's; a mantelpiece looking glass, framed in faded velvet, with mauve flowers painted on it and a retrieving dog, also done by the aunt; a papier-mâché clock, painted with gold paint, which had stopped; a nest of tea tables holding lucky slippers, cats, horseshoes, etc.; an oval table with pot containing a defunct primula in red crepe paper; a Second Empire circular mirror with eagle; six amateur oil paintings of horses and lunar landscapes, one of them good; an enormous cheap print of Jesus Christ pointing at His Sacred Heart; a plain mahogany table which served for an altar when they had a Station; and a card table for playing Spoil Five. The wallpaper was mildewed because of the stone, but it had been discovered that the pictures could be saved from the mildew by propping them away from the wall, with corks out of whisky bottles.

While on the subject of furniture, it would be fair to describe the dining room. It was only that they had been furnished at different periods, one of which was, for the time being, too recent to seem as hallowed as the other.

In the dining room, which suited the date of the house, there was a quiet, formal wallpaper, and a priceless Nelson sideboard with table and chairs to match. There were also: a lovely writing desk combined with book shelves, which had secret drawers (still a secret to Mrs. O'Callaghan) and oval-paned glass doors, most of the panes being broken; a good deal of imitation silver, wedding presents to Mikey and his bride; three attractive china plates commemorating a Eucharistic Congress, their Sacred Hearts exploding into flames like bombards; a set of Queen Anne teaspoons which Mr. White had rescued from the kitchen, where they had been put since some Woolworth spoons had been bought; a wireless set on a good nineteenth-century side table; a dead hydrangea on a bad twentieth-century circular table; a self-portrait of Mr. White, done in the drawing-room mirror, the flowered one; an imposing black marble clock broken by Mikey, as, indeed, all the clocks at Burkestown had been broken by him, his method of repair, after he had overwound them, being to insert a turkey feather through any visible aperture and to twiddle it about; an excellent carpet, firedogs, and nineteenth-century grate; five mezzotints after Morland and Constable; bookshelves containing the whole Everyman Library, imported by Mr. White; severe gray marble fireplace; and, on the Nelson sideboard, the Infant of Prague.

The house itself was of the late eighteenth century. It had belonged to a squireen who had expected his yearly invitation to Dublin Castle, and who had been a friend of a mythological Irish character called Major Sirr. It was orientated according to eighteenth-century ideas, so that no single point of the compass was satisfactory. The company rooms faced north, so that they were in perpetual gloom, but they did not face to the true north, for fear that any of the other walls might face to the true south. The wall which ought to have been south, the one which had the greenhouse, was in fact a bit to the southeast, so that it only took the sun until four o'clock in the afternoon in summer. Moreover, this partly south wall had been built with no windows, for fear that any of the rooms in the house might have been sunny or dry. The stone of which the walls were built made dryness impossible, but the orientation made assurance doubly sure.

The transference of the Wincharger to its temporary casing on the drawing-room chimney took two days. Luckily, the distance from the roof of the hay barn to the point of entry was the same as the distance from the chimney to that point, so that no alteration was necessary in the cable. The erection took two days because it was a constructive job, and in this case Pat Geraghty had to do everything twice.

The dismantling of the hay barn went faster,

because it was destructive. The advantage of destructive work was that Geraghty could not do it again. Once a corrugated sheet was off, it was done. Even if Mr. White had taken it off, Pat could scarcely put it on again in order to do the same thing. They started from the far end, next the cowsheds, so as to leave their line of retreat open.

Brownie deplored the barn. She could not climb from the table and chair to the fluted roof, and spent the time sitting in the yard, groaning with disapproval.

Mrs. O'Callaghan sent up tea to Mr. White at intervals of a few hours.

Mikey took the pony trap to Cashelmor, to do the shopping. His real object was to escape the harvest.

Philomena turned her attention to Mr. White's cravats, which he wore on Sundays with peculiar Victorian tiepins, and which her twenty-three brothers and sisters tied round their stomachs as a specific against lumbago.

Tommy Plunkett ran the farm as best he could.

When a sheet had been unbolted and lifted off, it was handed down to the Slane Meadow, which was the field behind the hay barn. The river Slane flowed at the bottom of this field, and Mr. White said that even if the Flood was to be augmented by a general subsidence of the earth's crust, yet it was likely to begin in the bed of the Slane, at least in its initial stages. This meadow was also clear of trees, which made it a suitable location for floating off the Ark, and therefore for building it there.

The roof was not bolted to the girders. It was secured to them by galvanized clips. These, with the nuts and bolts, were put aside for reassembly.

It took only a day to dismantle the roof. The next stage was to take down the arc-shaped girders, of which there were four.

They twisted strong hay ropes for this job, with a twister, as the ironmonger in Cashelmor had nothing stronger than rope reins. They began with the two middle girders, because the two outside ones thus gave them a natural scaffolding from which to sling them. When the middle girders were down, the outside ones completed the square of the framework at the top, and this was the next thing to tackle.

It was more difficult. They had to tie the remaining girders—those of the sides and ends—to the upright supports before unbolting them. Then they had to untie them at one end, and lower that end with a hay rope, after which they untied the other end, and lowered that. The girders weighed about a hundredweight, and could be carried round to the Slane Meadow by hand.

Finally the upright supports had to be sawed off without dropping them, and without killing the person who did the sawing. They did not like the idea of dropping cast iron eighteen feet to cobbles. It was a poser, how to get them cut and lowered.

In the end they had to go the whole hog, dismantle the barn completely, lower the uprights by slinging them from one another and from the roof of the cowshed, and saw them on the ground. It took two days extra, but it was worth it. They realized that they would have been forced to dismantle the whole thing sooner or later, in order to get the sheeting from the lower sides which was to be used to deck the Ark, when ready.

For the first few days the barn looked as if it had been bombed out. Then it got to look less and less as if it had ever been a barn at all. One day it was gone completely, and the yard was different. It was airy and strange. There was something missing, like the gap of an extracted tooth into which the owner puts his tongue with unfamiliar surprise.

CHAPTER
VIII

It was useless to discuss the tool list with Mikey and Mrs. O'Callaghan. Their horizon on the subject of tools was bounded by the only one they had. It was what they called a wrinch, and they used it a good deal on the lid of the churn. Its handle was slippery with milk products, turkey mash, and the natural greases of Mikey.

Obviously they would have to take the contents of the tool cupboard. They were to build a new world. But it was the farm machinery that was the puzzle, because of space.

A plough was inevitable, also a plain harrow with the swings for both. It seemed best not to take a spring-tooth harrow, for fear that the teeth would snap. Then there was other machinery, like the horse rake and the mowing machine, which would be bulky and might possibly be done without. Finally there were things like the horse roller, which had to be left behind, unless . . . Mr. White decided to take the mowing machine to pieces, so that it could be stored without wasting space. Then he saw that he would have to take a blacksmith's anvil, bellows, and vice. Next he concluded that he would ballast the Ark with iron rods, scrap iron, spare wheels of several sizes, and general materials of this sort. Finally he said that they might as well take the hayrake to pieces, and use that as ballast. He weakened toward the roller.

"When the Ark has landed," said he, "we will turn it the right way up and use it as a house. It will mean shifting the ballast as soon as we touch, so that she rolls over on her side, of her own accord. Then it ought not to be difficult to heave her, particularly if we can land on a slope. We shall have to peg her down. She will make a splendid house. You could not have a better one. I can take out a sheet or two for windows and doors. I suppose we can't take glass. . . .

"A pump!" he cried. "We shall need a pump during the voyage, in case she leaks, and it will come in useful afterward, if we dig a well. I am afraid a stirrup pump would not do. I will buy an ordinary well pump and fix it in the stern. Can you divine water, Mrs. O'Callaghan?"

"Pardon?"

"Are you a water diviner? A man who tells you where to dig for wells?"

She was tickled. As if she could tell you where to dig a well! Everybody knew that she could scarcely tell you anything. And besides, to imagine that she was a man!

"Well then," said Mr. White, "you are, but you don't know it. Everybody is. You only need to be shown."

It was blowing great guns outside, and the twilight was falling. It would have needed more than that to stop him. He went raging off to the top of the boithrin, where the hazels grew, and began hacking off a Y-shaped twig with his penknife, wishing that he had brought a slash hook.

("We must take a slash hook.")

Mrs. O'Callaghan was pretending that she had forgotten about water divining when he came back. She knew what she was in for. To distract his attention from the subject, in which she foresaw disaster, she had started writing her tool list with the greatest industry, and had put down "Wrinch" three times.

He was having none of that.

"Now then, Mrs. O'Callaghan, come along out to the Lawn, and I'll teach you how to divine water."

"It does be going to rain."

"No, it won't. Come on. It's quite easy."

"Me shoes . . ."

"The grass is dry."

"Won't it do tomorrow, when we have the light?"

"No, no, no. It won't take a minute. Everybody can do it, only they don't know how."

Mrs. O'Callaghan had a fatal weakness on the subject of learning things, and it was coming over her now. She was able to hypnotize herself in the belief that they could not possibly be done.

One of the most terrible evenings they had ever spent at Burkestown had happened several years before, when Mr. White, as a newcomer, had started showing them conjuring tricks. He knew only four, which were of the simplest description. For instance, he would place his fountain pen between his two hands, palms together, with the pen held in the two angles between thumb and forefinger of each hand. Then, with a sudden twisting movement, he would display the pen held in the same position, but thumbs downward. To make it sound difficult, he had to say in the patter that he had "pushed his thumbs through the pen." As the O'Callaghans had no means of knowing what the devil he was trying to do with the pen in any case, and, moreover, as they believed implicitly that he had pushed his thumbs through it, since he said so, the position had gradually become more and more divorced from reality; particularly when Mr.

White had tried to show Mrs. O'Callaghan how to do it herself. To begin with, he had just done it a little slower, so that she could see the trick. Then he had done it very slowly indeed, twenty or thirty times over. Growing obstinate, and determined to amuse, instruct, or elevate the mind, he had thrust the wretched pen into Mrs. O'Callaghan's hands, and, seizing these in his own, had twisted her into every conceivable position, in the effort to make her understand. Mrs. O'Callaghan, who did not know how to do the thing because in the first place she did not know what she was trying to do, and who was already far advanced in her characteristic hypnosis, had begun to sweat. Beads of perspiration had stood out on her eyebrows and rolled down the sides of her nose, while Mr. White, with ghastly pleasantries, had twisted her wrists and dislocated her fingers and told her how easy it was. Occasionally he had halted, gasped, taken a sip of whisky to revive himself, and hurled his energies once more into the breach. More and more complications had transpired. It had become obvious that, although Mrs. O'Callaghan was able to tell her right hand from her left, in the sense that one of them was on one side of her and one of them was on the other—and even this she was rapidly forgetting—yet she was not able to name them accurately when flustered. It had seemed that she did possess some mnemonic on the subject, as landlubbers do for distinguishing the starboard from the port, but in moments of stress she was unable to remember the mnemonic, which had hampered her as a student of legerdemain. Mr. White growing momently more drunk and more desperate, as they wrestled together through the hours of a night which seemed to both of them as if it could never end, and Mrs. O'Callaghan, by now terrified, half insensible and covered with a mixture of ink and perspiration, had switched from one to another of the four conjuring tricks with bewildering speed, in the effort to discover one at least that he would be able to teach her; but in vain. He had explained that he had not really passed his thumbs through the pen, which had so confused her that she had ceased to repose any faith in any of his statements on the subject. They had stood opposite each other, like image and object in a mirror, manhandling the corks, matches, and fountain pens which were Mr. White's materials, and, when he had treated her as an image, she had treated him as an object—lifting the opposite hand—while, when he had quickly switched over to being the object, she, as quickly, had caught up with the original intention and had treated him as the image. She had said how silly she was, how wonderful it was, what a head Mr. White had, and would you believe it? She had poured with sweat, dropped things, become entangled with her fingers, and laughed with wild propitiation, like some elderly Ophelia forced to hand out rosemary, rue, matches, corks, and fountain pens. Mikey had sided against her, asking angrily why didn't she do as the gintleman said, and pass her thumbs through the pin? Suddenly—and how strangely, in this world, comedy verges on tragedy at a clap—Mr. White had seen that her hands were trembling. The poor, long, red fingers, which had scrubbed for so many years so many kitchen tables so in—efficiently, had been trembling with fear and misery and humiliation. In another minute, she would have begun to cry.

It was things like this that made him love her so much.

She, for her part, it is curious to relate, loved Mr. White for his whiskers. They made him look just like St. Joseph, she said.

Well, so now it was water divining.

She stood twisting her hands in her apron, in the gusty twilight, while Mr. White delivered a short homily and gave a demonstration.

"We won't go near the well—because that would not be fair—but we will go over here to the beech trees, and see if we can find any there."

Three-quarters of the farm stood on a wide strip of yellow clay, about eighteen inches below the surface, like a saucer, so that Mr. White was able to find water practically wherever he stood, which made it a good place for divining.

"Now, I'll show you first of all how it is done. You take this twig in the palms of your hands, like this, and you put your thumbs tight on the tops of the Y, like this. You hold your arms out straight in front of you. Then you give the twig a twist with your wrists, like this, so that the foot of the Y stands up straight in the air. There.

"Everybody can do it," he added reassuringly. "People think that it is only diviners who can do it, but the faculty is universal. As soon as you show them properly, they find that they can do it themselves. I have taught dozens of people. I never failed to teach anybody yet.

"Now the next thing is to walk along steadily and collectedly, putting your feet down firmly on the earth so that the power can flow up through them, keeping your thumbs tight on the butts of the rod, concentrating your attention and not walking fast.

"With me," said Mr. White, pacing off into the darkness, concentrating his attention, keeping his thumbs tight, putting his feet down firmly, and gradually disappearing in gloom and gale, "the twig always bends inward. With other people it sometimes bends away. You can hold as tight as you like, in fact the tighter the better, but the twig will bow, even if it has to twist its own bark off to do it. Look, it is beginning to come already. You see, I am holding it as tight as I can. You can see my hands trembling. Watch closely, and you will see that I cannot possibly be twisting it myself. It is not a trick. It really happens, and you can't stop it. Look, you can see a little wrinkle in the bark, where it is forcing against my grip. Do you see?"

He turned round like a weather cock, arms rigid, twig erect, anxious to give Mrs. O'Callaghan the benefit of this pleasing spectacle.

She had fled.

"Good God," cried Mr. White, dashing his twig to the earth, "she won't even try water divining!"

Then he picked the twig up and went off to do some by himself.

Coming home in the moonlight, through the gate which Mikey used to have to climb over, he did not want to throw away the hazel. He hung it on the hasp of the gate, thinking hopefully: Perhaps Pat Geraghty would like to be taught?

The light was lit in the kitchen and Mrs. O'Callaghan was writing on her list of wrinches. She had tied a piece of red flannel round her neck, and hoped to explain her conduct by saying that she had suddenly got a sore throat. She was saved all explanation, however, for Mr. White had noticed the noise of a tractor, working by the moon in the press of harvest, as he came in.

"What a pity that we can't take a tractor! We could use it for a saw bench, and to thresh, and even to make electric light. But it is a question of fuel. We cannot possibly expect to land on a petroleum well, and we would not have time to prospect for one, and in any case I don't know how to control a well or how to refine the oil. But, by Jove, we will take the Wincharger! There will still be the wind, at any rate, and it will be a great thing for our children . . ."

He stopped suddenly.

"It will be a great thing, anyway, to carry over electric light from the old world to the new. We will fix it on the Ark itself, to give us light during the voyage, and even if its gets worn out eventually, it will be there as an object lesson for future generations, who have more leisure, to copy or to renovate. Come to think of it, I have some money in the bank, which will be perfectly useless after the Flood, so I may as well spend it before. I will buy a new Wincharger, the strongest one we can get, and we will keep the old one in reserve. Then we will fix up the new one on the Ark with a refrigerator—what voltages do they run to, I wonder? A refrigerator will be of enormous use to us, for storing dead fish in and things like that—we shall be able to fish during the trip—and we are to remember that we shall have nothing but our own stores to live on, until the first harvest comes in. And, talking of that, we must take plenty of fish-hooks and fishing line and spinners, and we ought to take a net. We may land near the sea. Indeed, if we do not land near the sea it is going to be pretty difficult to keep going till harvest. We have not only ourselves, but also the beasts to feed. I wonder if the strawberry netting from the garden would do, or whether I shall have to buy a proper seine?"

Mikey said: "Does it be hard to combine water?"

"To combine water?"

"Like what ye said."

It all came back to him in a flash. He looked accusingly at Mrs. O'Callaghan, noted her red flannel—guessing its purpose instinctively, from long practice—counted ten, and decided to leave her to her own remorse. Besides, he now had Mikey.

"No," he said, "Mikey, it is perfectly easy. I'll teach you how to do it in the morning."

"Does it hurt?"

"Not at all. In fact, the reverse. You'll see. You're the very man for the job."

Mikey blushed with pleasure.

"I wrote down 'Wrinch,' " he said proudly.

"Well done. We will take the wrench by all means. Did you write down anything else?"

Mikey had excelled himself, and knew it.

"I put churn and separator and stone and growbar and coal chisel and binder twine and staples and knitted wire and forks and spade and shovel and harness and britching and copper rivets!"

"Let's take them one by one, and see."

Soon even Mrs. O'Callaghan had been restored to favor, for suggesting needles, and all three of them were deep in a mine of assorted implements, from which Mr. White occasionally cast up such curiosities as electric bulbs, chamber pots, tin openers, reflex Devon minnows, flint and steel, sheep shears, spare spectacles, and tooth paste.

Mikey, by the way, had never brushed his teeth in his life; yet he had five brown fangs still in use, and only one of them wobbled.

CHAPTER
IX

Since the roof of the hay barn had to be assembled upside down, and since it would need to have the keel fastened under it and would in any case roll on its side, unless supported, because it was trough-shaped—and since the corrugated sheets now had to be clipped under the girders—it was necessary to make a simple scaffolding. They used the three-by-three from the garage store to make props for the four girder arcs at the right height above the ground, allowing for the keel. The keel was to be made from the spare or sawed-off lengths of the uprights, which were a foot in width, and these were laid along the ground between the props. It had been decided to attach the keel with galvanized clips, to save making boltholes which might leak. Then the corrugated sheets were clipped on one by one, from girders to keel, and bolted together, with the nuts inside. The heavier the structure grew, the more it had its own frame to support it, so that the props of three-by-three finally remained only in order to keep it from rolling over.

The sheets at the far end were not put on, as the large animals would have to be led in at that end, up a ramp, at the last moment, before the Ark could be closed for her journey.

These things took longer than they take to tell—

for the shipwrights were back at the constructive stage, when everything had to be done twice—and Mr. White had time for the humanities.

A moment's quiet reflection had made him see that it was useless to teach Mikey water divining, however universal the faculty, because the latter had scarcely any faculties, whether universal or not. It would have to be Geraghty.

He fetched the hazel guiltily and tried to pretend that he did not want to show anybody anything.

"Did you ever see any water divining?"

"No, sorr," said Geraghty. "It can't be done."

"But it can be done. I can do it myself. So can . . ."

"Ye think ye can do it, sorr, being a gintleman, but that's where they have ye codded.

"No man," added Geraghty reverently, casting his eyes to heaven, "but the Man Above, is able to lay his finger on water. And I'll tell ye for why . . ."

"But I know I can do it. I've done it hundreds of times. I can show you . . ."

"Ye think ye can show me, sorr, no doubt. I wouldn't be doubting the word of a gintleman."

He again cast his eyes to heaven, either in honor of the given word or else of the extinct gentry of the twenty-six counties.

"But the Houly Spirit av God has ordained otherwise, sorr, as a gintleman of your eddication should be able to tell. Vengeance is mine, saith the Lord, I will repay. Nor must any man give credance unto soothsayers.

"They shall sit," added Geraghty, "every man under his vine and under his fig tree."

"Yes, yes. But what has all this to do with water divining? I tell you I can do it with this rod I have in my hand. So could you. I could teach you in a minute."

Geraghty shook his head indulgently. At the

present stage of his life he enjoyed laboring for Mr. White, who was the only man with whom he had been able to work. This was for the much repeated reason that the latter was a gintleman. Gintlemen were notoriously childish in the manual occupations, so that Geraghty was able, as it were, to indulge his employer, if he absolutely insisted on doing something himself, and he did not have to be constantly reproving him for doing things wrong. He did not expect a gintleman to do things right.

"Sure," he said, "why wouldn't ye be able for it, wid yer little stick? Let ye go now and play wid it, till I have me girder clipped."

Mr. White stamped his foot.

"I don't want to play with any sticks. I'm telling you that this stick would bend over in my hand if I walked over water, and so it would in your hand too, if you did."

"Why would I be walking about all day wid a stick? I have me living, sorr, begging your pardon, to earn be the sweat of me brow. Now a gintleman . . ."

"Oh, God damn these gintlemen," cried Mr. White passionately. He threw the hazel on the dung heap and went off to discover Mrs. O'Callaghan.

She was in the kitchen.

He opened the shutter automatically, to let the light fall on the fire, as he did every time he entered the room, a process which she reversed every time he left it.

He said: "Mrs. O'Callaghan, I am going to buy an electric cooker which will work off the new wind machine. It will save all the space which we should need to use for fuel, if we tried to cook in the Ark by other means. Now I want you to imagine that you are going to Cashelmor to do your week's shopping, but, instead of a week, it is to be for a year. Do you understand? Imagine that you are going to do a year's shopping in Cashelmor, and make out a shopping list for it. All the things you would need in the kitchen, to keep you going for a year. Salt, tea, pepper, sugar, soap, flour, and all that. Not just a pound of them, or whatever you usually get, but enough for a whole year. We shan't be able to take it all, but when you have the list we will go over it and whittle it down. Do you think you can do that?"

"I can't do it till I have me dinner cooked," said Mrs. O'Callaghan, in some alarm.

"No hurry. Any time will do."

"Will I put down coal?"

"No," he said, "not with an electric cooker."

He stood gloomily at the window, suddenly feeling old and pointless. She will do it all wrong, he thought. She will take too much tea and too little salt, and the salt will be allowed to melt into mush as usual. Neither of them can do any arithmetic. What is the good of trying? What is the good of scrambling about on this wretched Ark with bolts and things, when everything will go wrong? What is the good of nagging at poor Mikey to get the harvest in or at Mrs. O'Callaghan to keep the shutters open? They are both far too old to change. For that matter, what is the good of doing anything with the Irish, who won't even try water divining? What are they? Just a rag bag of every defeated nation since the dawn of prehistory, driven into this accursed rain cloud of an island as the last refuge for incapacity. They think that the sunlight puts fires out and the moon changes the weather and God knows what else. I suppose they think that the moon is a kind of phosphorescent balloon which gets gradually blown up and deflated. They have no idea of the earth's shadow or of geography or of anything else. The only good thing is that they murder one another at a great rate. How many murders did we have last month? There was the man who threw his wife into a well with a turkey, and the man who chopped up his brother and buried him in a bog, and the man who decapitated his grandmother with a hatchet, and ... and ... Always pointless, too, and so badly done. The whole island is strewn with blunt instruments which the murderer has forgotten to conceal. Professional assassins, all over the world, are Irishmen or Italians. Chicago, everywhere. I suppose they'll murder me before they've finished. For the sake of a cigarette card or something. It's lucky Mikey is timid. He'd be afraid to make a bad shot the first time, and get hurt himself. Not that he dislikes me. It would be a sudden whim, as usual. . . .

What's the good of struggling with it all? It isn't only the O'Callaghans, it's the whole island. You might as well try to reform the Alps. And why reform them, anyway? Why transplant human life at all, in this ridiculous Ark? Why not leave it to be exterminated?

Why live, thought Mr. White, for that matter? I'm sure I don't know why we take such trouble to do so. It's all rheumatism, and filling up forms.

He went out to the garden.

Mikey was waiting for him at a safe distance from the beehives. He had found the hazel rod and was tongue-tied with longing, doubt, modesty, or apprehension. He hung his head, peeped coyly sideways across his red nose like a parrot asking to have its poll scratched, simpered, rubbed the ground with his toe, put his finger in his mouth, rotated on his heel, flapped his coattails, and blushingly displayed the hazel.

"Well, Mikey."

Mikey giggled.

Mr. White knew exactly where they would fail. It would be at the raising of the twig, which required a simple contortion. But the little man wanted to try, which was a virtue worth encouragement. Besides, he was like a child asking for a treat. Water divining, like knitting, had proved to be contagious.

"Very well," he said sadly. "We'll go to the beech trees and have a try."

When the first part of the demonstration was over, he proceeded to dual control.

"Now, Mikey, we'll do it together. Take hold of this arm of the Y with your left hand. No, the other one. Put your thumb tight on the cut surface. No, your thumb. No, the other thumb. Look, let me do it."

He seized all Mikey's fingers and thumbs, and began sorting them out in a determined way, applying one here and one there, curling them round the twig and training them in various directions, like the branches of a creeper. They were red and clammy.

"That's right. Now, you hold tight like that, with your left hand on the left-hand fork. I'll take the right-hand fork in my right hand, and then we'll join our spare hands together, to complete the circuit. You and I will have hold of one branch of the fork each, and I shall hold your right hand in my left hand, so that the current is closed in. No, the other hand. That's right."

Mr. White grasped the damp paw manfully—he had once kept a pet toad—and the two stood side by side, hand in hand, holding the hazel out between them.

"Now we've got to lift the point of the rod in the air, Mikey. It means giving a twist of your wrist, like this."

Mr. White twisted his wrist, but as Mikey, of

course, did not twist his wrist—in order to demonstrate to himself how to twist his wrist—the necessary contortion remained frozen halfway, like the Laocoön.

"Wait a bit. Keep hold of the twig, Mikey, but let go of my spare hand. No, let go. No, hold the twig. That's right. Now then."

Mr. White, having freed his left hand, forced the twig upright by main strength with it. He and Mikey revolved for a bit, like sword dancers passing under their blades in a morris, and, after a half pirouette, remained side by side with the twig upright. They joined hands once more.

All this time Mikey had watched the twig in silence, without looking at anything else.

"There. Now stand still for a minute and feel yourself. Feel the ground under your feet, and the force coming through my hand into yours, and think about the twig. Hold it tight. Don't think about anything else. Just feel us both together and the ground under us and the twig in front. Do you feel it?"

"Yes," whispered Mikey.

"Then we'll walk forward slowly, a few steps. No, slowly. Put your feet down firm, and walk with me."

They moved off jerkily, at a sort of goose step, like storm troopers in a three-legged race.

"Stop. We're going too fast. Don't prance so, Mikey. Go along smoothly and don't think so much about your feet. Think about my hand and the twig. Now, slowly and smoothly . . ."

Like red Indians on the warpath, crouching slightly, they advanced stealthily behind their twig, eyes fixed, palms glued together by Mikey's sweat, without another thought in the world.

"It's beginning. Stand still. Do you feel it?"

He could only nod.

"Three more steps then. Quietly. Here it comes. Hold it as tight as you can. Don't let it come, Mikey. Hold on. You can see it is not me that's moving it. Now another step. Hold tight. Now another. Stand still. We're over water now, Mikey. Don't let it come. Now another. There!"

The twig turned right over and pointed to the ground.

"It turnded over," said Mikey.

He was like a man in church.

"Yes."

"I couldn' stop it."

"No."

"It turnded itself."

"Yes."

"Lor!"

"Now you must do it alone, Mikey. Come back where we started from."

Mr. White was determined to strike while the iron was hot.

"Take hold of both arms of the twig this time. That's right. No, not the point. That's better. Now look, Mikey, you've got to get the twig pointed up somehow. Keep hold of it, whatever you do, and, by God, I'll get the point up for you if it kills me. Keep your elbows straight, Mikey. Keep your arms out. As I lift, let the backs of your hands go face inward toward each other. Let them come. No, the backs. Keep hold. Don't let go. Let your thumbs down, Mikey. It's coming. That's right. Keep on. We're winning. By heaven, it's up!"

He stepped back cautiously, ready to dash in again if Mikey showed signs of falling to pieces; but he held.

"You have it!"

Mikey stood—rigid, red, unable to breathe, crucified to his twig, determined to succeed or die.

"Good. Now stay still as you are and think about

the twig. Think about the ground under your feet. Don't think about anything else. Just feel yourself there."

They waited.

"Do you feel firm?"

A nod.

"Walk slowly then. A few steps. Think about the twig. Not too fast. That's right. Mikey, you're going to do it. Now stop. Now a step. Go as you like, Mikey, if you feel yourself right. Don't mind me. Go on. Go alone!"

Step for step, pace by pace, Mikey like a sleep-walker and Mr. White concentrating terrific forces upon him (walking crabwise, on the balls of his feet, as if about to spring), they advanced toward the beeches.

Mikey's mouth opened.

The hazel was bowing.

Mikey thought he had spoken, but nobody could have heard a word.

They panted audibly.

They paused.

They advanced.

The hazel was a sagging arch.

Mikey's wrists were trembling.

They stopped.

The rod turned over and pointed to the ground.

Mr. White took the twig away from him and shook him by the hand. He pumped it up and down. He kept on shaking it and patting Mikey, with tears in his eyes. He turned away and blew his nose.

It had been done. It had been accomplished. *Ite, missa est.* All those hours with knitting needles and pokers and matches and fountain pens and God knows what else—*Nunc dimittis* . . . He had had faith, and he had won through. He had taught the

O'Callaghans. To strive, to seek, to find, and not to yield.

Mikey began talking twenty to the dozen. He was transfigured.

"It turnded."

"Yes."

"I done it."

"Yes."

"It turnded right over."

"Yes."

"Ye can't stop it."

"No."

"It be's the water."

"Yes."

"Everybody can do it."

"Yes"

"I can do it."

"Yes."

"I done it be meself."

"Yes."

"Did ye see it turn?"

"Yes."

"Can I do it again?"

"Yes, Mikey, hundreds of times. Do it again now, quickly, so that you'll remember how."

They did it again and again and again. After the third time, he could twist the point up for himself. They were in the seventh heaven.

At the dinner hour Mikey asked timidly: "May I keep the twig for me own?"

"It's yours, Mikey, forever. And after dinner I'll cut you twenty more, for spares."

CHAPTER
X

Mrs. O'Callaghan said: "Thim piano roses does be pretty."

Brownie had got exasperated with lists, and was sitting on a kitchen table, on Mr. White's, to prevent him from writing. He was searching for fleas on her, with the nib of his fountain pen.

He replied: "I don't know whether peonies grow from seed or from tubers. Tubers would be bulky to store. But you are quite right, Mrs. O'Callaghan, about flowers. I am glad you suggested them. After all, dash it, we need not make the new world entirely utilitarian. It would be a poor lookout for our ch . . . It would be a poor lookout if everything had to be either oats or cabbages. I see no reason at all why we should not take some color with us, a little beauty and culture if we can get it, particularly as seeds take up so little space. I will write to Sir James Mackey's and get them to put up an assortment of flower seeds of all sorts. And, so far as that goes, I mean Culture, I was thinking last night about what books to take. People who are going to be shipwrecked on desert islands usually take the Bible and Shakespeare, I believe; but, as we are a good Catholic household, we have no Bible, and in any case I think the *Encyclopædia Britannica* would be more useful. To re-create a culture we should need that, and I wonder if we dare take the *Dictionary of National Biography* instead of Shakespeare?"

He tapped his teeth with the other end of the pen for some time, then said with determination: "I will not believe that the Archangel Michael is only interested in Winchargers. If we took the whole Everyman Library, and the whole Penguin Library, we could probably get them into a pair of tea chests. For that matter, I don't suppose I have more than a couple of thousand books all told, and they would not take up as much room as a horse. Which is the more important, a horse or the Library of Alexandria? Probably a horse. But we will damned well take the books as well."

"Mrs. O'Callaghan," said he later, balancing his list on Brownie's back because she would not let him write anywhere else, "do you know, this is a tougher job than it looked when we started. Do you think you could learn to eat grass?"

Mrs. O'Callaghan was feeling mean about having let Mikey get ahead of her as a water combiner, and she was determined to learn the next thing suggested—but grass . . . She gulped, working her fingers convulsively.

"We could start with young grass," he said enticingly, "in salads and so on. We could work up to it gradually, don't you think?"

"Nothing but grass?"

"It would only be for a time."

"But me stomach . . ."

"It's like this. Our Ark will be only sixteen yards long and eight yards wide. Inside, there will be room to stand up, or a good bit over, actually, because we decided not to shorten the side sheets after all. Now we have got to pack into this, of large animals, at least one mare and one cow and one sow, with their young males, and ourselves, and several other smaller animals, and our materi-

als for a new world, and our farm machinery, and
food for all of us for a year. It is that damned
horse that is going to gobble up such a lot. Now, it
is evident that the sooner we can procure a harvest of some sort out of the slime, the sooner we
shall have the horse and cow provided for, and
that means saving space on their provisions. It is
going to be touch and go in any case, when you
think of our provisions as well. I was trying to
decide what sort of harvest would come in quick-
est, with most return, and I have a feeling that
grass is the answer. Mustard and cress would hardly
be sustaining. It seems to me that you can grow
more grass more quickly than anything else, and
therefore that we shall have to take an enormous
amount of grass seed and sow it the moment we
land. With luck we could let Nancy and the cow
begin to eat it after a couple of months, which
would shorten the time on provisions most wonderfully. That's what made me wonder if we could
eat grass ourselves. If we could live on grass for a
bit, until harvest, there would be all the more
room in the Ark for future luxuries. I know for a
fact that several people have lived on grass. . . .

"Have you," he demanded suddenly, turning
upon her, "the same number of stomachs as a
cow?"

"Me stomach . . ."

"It all depends on how many stomachs you have.
I am sure I remember hearing that a horse had
one less, or one more, I can't remember which. It
is simply a matter of combustion. I must find out.

"Of course," added Mr. White graciously, "we
shall not need to graze. We could pick it first, and
even boil it a little if you liked."

"Nittles," said Mrs. O'Callaghan faintly.

She had often eaten nettles, which, she claimed,
were good for her blood.

"That's a good idea. I wonder. They grow fast. The danger lies in taking weeds into the new world. But if we were exceedingly careful to reap them young, before there was any chance of their seeding, and to reap the whole lot . . .

"Do you know, Mrs. O'Callaghan, there is one feature of this new world which I am worried about, and that is the matter of domestic animals and domestic vegetables. Things that have been made domestic are much less hardy than wild things. We shall have a world full of cabbages and cows, no doubt, and there won't be any thistles or tigers in it, but the danger is that what we do take, the tame things, will die off too easily. . . . Where's Mikey?"

"Gone down to Jimmy Murphy's, wid his twig."

"Why?"

"Sure, he's gone to teach him how to combine water. He was combining it all the afternoon, wid himself. The barley's shed and the oats is shedding, Tommy Plunkett says; but there you are, Mr. White, what can I do? It's the Holy Will av God."

"Shed!"

"Shed, Mr. White."

Mrs. O'Callaghan's general principle about the disasters of the farm was to ignore them if they were remediable and to go into a closed circular flap about them if they were not. Thus, if Mikey proposed to buy a "seven-year-old" pony, unseen, broken winded, aged thirty-three, a stumbler, paying five times its price without demur, because he was frightened of the dealer, Mrs. O'Callaghan took the matter calmly, because it was or could have been remediable. But if it rained continuously throughout the harvest, as it generally did, a fact which nobody on this earth could remedy, then Mrs. O'Callaghan would spend the time running round like a chicken with its head cut off, putting the blame on Mikey. Her circular flap generally took the circuit: "It has me stomach at me—Me a slave—The men play on Mikey—I'll set the land—It has me stomach at me." The idea must have been that a remediable disaster called for remedy—and therefore had to be ignored, for fear of having to remedy it—while an irremediable disaster called for no positive action and could therefore be recognized without danger. Also Mrs. O'Callaghan may have felt that any remedies applied by her, other than a circular flap, would probably increase the disaster, owing to the corner in Heads which had been established by the Holy Will of God.

The shedding of the harvest had been a remediable disaster.

"Good heavens!" cried Mr. White, who flapped on opposite principles. "And we shall need the grain to take with us! What the devil has Mikey been doing? I told him to get on with the harvest, with Tommy. Has he fixed up with anybody to bring a binder?"

"He was going a Tuesday, only he had to do the shopping."

"And Wednesday and Thursday? And Friday we were water divining. And even if he goes tomorrow, we shall have to wait the week end!"

"Well, there ye are then. It's not me fault, Mr. White. What can I do?"

"Oh, God! I suppose I shall have to knock off work on the Ark and try to get the wheat in myself. That's not shed yet, is it?"

"I didn't hear it was."

"Mikey must go tomorrow and ask if Francey can come on Monday. If he can't get Francey, he must get somebody else. Tell him that if he can't get anybody he need not come home himself."

"Nobody knows what it is," said Mrs. O'Callaghan placidly, "except thim that has to go through wid it."

"For that matter, he could be trying to get a binder this minute. . . . But he has to go round playing with twigs."

"That's the way it goes, Mr. White. I suppose it does be the Holy . . ."

"Yes, yes. It's the Holy Will of God. Anyway, we can't do anything about it till Mikey comes back, so let's get on with this list.

"Shed!" continued Mr. White. "The barley shed and the oats shedding, and nobody cares a damn. . . . But the list, the list! Where had we got to on the list?"

"We have the garden vegetables down, and the packet of flowers, and grass, and nittles . . ."

"And there's the question of growing tobacco for Mikey, if we come down in a suitable climate. So far as that goes, I think I'll write to the Botanical Gardens at Kew, and ask them if they can spare us a selection of peculiar seeds. For all we know, we shall be dropped in an ice age, for that matter, and won't be able to grow anything but sphagnum moss. I wish we had a reindeer. . . .

"It will cost money," cried Mr. White. "We shall have to pay for what we need. Luckily I can lay out the little I have, as it won't be any use after the Flood, and, by Jove, why shouldn't we sell the farm? It won't be any good to us afterward, even if we ever find it again, and, if we did find it again, it would be ours anyway, whether we had sold it or not, because there would be nobody else to claim it. Mrs. O'Callaghan, do you think it would be unfair to sell a farm to somebody, knowing that it was going to be destroyed by Flood a few weeks later?"

"I don't think Mikey would want to sell the farm. He had it from his Anty."

"So far as that goes," said Mr. White, paying no attention to this nonsense, "the purchaser himself would be destroyed in the Flood too. His money would be no good to him then. He may just as well give us the money for the farm, and be drowned, as not give us the money for the farm, and be drowned. I mean, he will be just as happy with the farm, for the few weeks remaining to him, as he would have been happy with the money in those weeks. . . . And besides, what is selling? It is a contract, I suppose, only conterminous with the duration of the thing sold. . . ."

"But we couldn't sell the farm, Mr. White. Supposing thim Floods didn't come?"

"Nonsense. If the Flood does not come, why did the Archangel tell us it would? You must have Faith, Mrs. O'Callaghan, Faith. And the reason why we want money is this: We want to take the best possible materials for a new world. For instance, if we had a few thousand pounds extra, we could afford to take two or three first-class wind machines, which would work a saw bench for us and all sorts of things. Also this matter of space will mean that we must take everything in its most concentrated form, and that will cost money.

"Look at the cow, now, and Nancy. We ought to take oil cake to feed them on, to save room, but we can't get it. Well then, we shall have to make some other concentrated food, even if we have to make it at some expense. What is the most concentrated food? Cows chew the cud and horses do not. It will need to have something chewable in it, for the cow. Do you think we could make a sort of sandwich out of hay, chocolate, grated carrots, cod-liver oil, and so forth? We could pour them over the hay, and press it. . . . I wish I knew about vitamins. There seem to be so many of them, and I believe they don't stand sunlight, and anyway I suppose they will soon be inventing something else. It might have to be sugar-coated, to keep out the sunlight. Probably laboratory made. Very expensive. I am glad you suggested selling the farm. And on polar expeditions they always take pemmican. We must take some pemmican. What is pemmican?"

"It be's a kind of religious bird."

"Yes. Well, the main point is that we shall need as much money as possible, so that we can take compressed foods and fine tools. It is quality we shall have to aim for, as we have no room for quantity, and that's where the money will come in.

"So far as that goes," continued Mr. White, brightening "it won't matter much about the harvest being spoiled, because we can buy grain with the farm money. And, by the way, grain itself is a bulky food. We must only take what we need for the actual sowing and the rest must go in the form of flour, which is more compressed. Do you think we could live on flour and cod-liver oil, in a sort of porridge?"

He was so pleased with all these ideas that, without waiting for an answer, he began playing a game with Brownie in which he was supposed to be a flea. He put his head down low over the kitchen table, on which she was lying with her back to him, and cautiously advanced his nose until the very tip of it was tickling the silky hairs on her back. This made Brownie jump, the first time, as it was an excellent imitation, and Mr. White cried out exultantly: "I'm a flea! I'm a flea!" It amused Brownie too, and they went on playing it for some time, until they both happened to jump at the same moment, and knocked their heads together.

Mr. White fell back dazed. It had started his brain spinning again, however.

"We must take some rice. I anticipate that one good result of the Flood will be to make the slime unusually prolific, like the Nile, so we must certainly take rice. Whether forty days under sea water will kill the trees or not, I don't know. But we had better take the seeds or slips of trees in case. Fortunately the trunks of the old trees will remain, whether they are dead or not, and these will serve as fuel and so on for many generations, while the seed trees grow, because there will be so few humans to use them up."

"There does be James Rafferty in Cashelmor has seven daughters," said Mrs. O'Callaghan hopefully, "that was taught the typewriting and the voilin."

He was saved from reply by the entry of Mikey, which was sensational.

With bloody nose, coatless, weeping bitterly, clutching a broken hazel, the latter tottered in and began to bleed over one of the kitchen tables.

For some mysterious reason there were five tables in the kitchen, and Mrs. O'Callaghan's main object in life was to scrub these, wash the stone floor, or polish the grate with spittle and ashes. She seldom had time for other interests.

They gave Mikey a soup plate to bleed in, and put the scullery key, which was enormous, down his back.

It was a matter of hours before the full story had been sobbed out, but, when it had been pieced together eventually, it was something like this:

It appeared that Mikey had spent the afternoon combing water on the farm—while the harvest shed. He had visited every field, combining plenty of it in each of them, until, when tea was over, he had felt a need, as Mr. White had felt before him, to display the talent on a more public stage—by teaching somebody else. It had either been that, or else that teaching, like knitting and water divining, had proved to be contagious.

Mikey, therefore, had gone down to the Slane Meadow, not to Murphy's, for there he expected to find a postman whose name was Vincent Quin. He had expected to find him there because Vincent was a keen fisherman who kept on slogging away at the reluctant salmon of the Slane until the very end of the season.

Mikey had found him there, as expected, trying to catch a particular salmon on the greased line.

When one comes to think of it, Mr. White must have spread an unsettling influence for some distance round Burkestown, for it was he who had taught the postman to fish with the greased line. It was not that Mr. White knew how to do this himself, but he had read a book on the subject. Vincent was using the art at a third remove from reality. He was, however, an enterprising and excitable character, not unlike his teacher in some respects, and he was quite pleased to fish with the greased line, and he was a suitable candidate for the art of combining. He wore spectacles and had a wooden leg.

Mikey had approached the postman, twig in hand, and had watched respectfully while he navigated the three flies along the almost motionless surface of the Slane for the fiftieth time. The salmon which Vincent was trying to amuse was, like most of the few salmon in the Slane, a hardened veteran who had been pricked some sixteen times on his way up the river, and neither he nor Vincent was particularly hopeful about each other by then.

Consequently, Mikey had managed to sell the idea of water combining pretty easily.

Mr. Quin had placed his rod in a sally bush, to keep the greasy line off the grass, and had left the extra-long cast, which Mr. White had tied for him, to flutter its three hooks in the air.

Mikey had given two or three exhibitions of combining, managing to detect the presence of the Slane in every case, and then, skipping the stage of dual control, had urged Vincent to combine some water for himself.

Unfortunately, owing to his bad eyesight, or perhaps through some racial handicap shared with Mikey, Vincent had proved unable to erect the twig. Mikey had showed him again, several times, and it seemed to have been at this stage that he had taken the fatal step of *trying to explain* to Vincent how the twig should be erected. While the accomplishment had been left in the unconscious layers of Mikey's intelligence, it had somehow managed to look after itself; but the strain of dragging it into consciousness had produced desperate consequences. The virtue had begun to drain out of Mikey rapidly. The more he had explained to Vincent, the less he had understood himself.

Growing uneasy, indeed beginning to grow terrified, Mikey had remembered the touchstone of dual control, and, at this late stage, had unwisely attempted to make Vincent erect the twig by doing it with him. They had struggled together for some time, like Siamese twins in disagreement, crying out advice, encouragement, or admonition, and had gradually approached the fishing rod in the excitement of the bout. At last, after four or five unusually vigorous *gargouillades* and a *tour en l'air,* they had emerged from a double half nelson right under the rod, and had stood there, back to back, in a dazed condition, still holding the rod, like ticktack men in a catalepsy. It had been Vincent who first realized that they had managed to hook themselves together in this position, by means of the three salmon flies, and he had immediately cried out in a warning tone: "Don't stir! Don't stir!" This had been unnecessary, however, as they were unable to stir. The flies had taken a firm hold of both their jackets, high up in the small of the back, in the one place which neither of them could reach for himself. Nor, of course, since they were attached to each other back to back, could either of them reach the other's. They had remained like this for some time, still holding out the twig, but losing their self-control and showing a tendency to upbraid one another on general subjects. Mikey had called the postman a faggot, possibly in allusion to his wooden leg, and the postman had called Mikey a bloody gom. The postman had been the first to have the idea of freeing himself by taking off his coat, but their spare arms—they still held the twig—were hooked together by one of the droppers, and this had meant that Mikey must move his arm backward in order to let the postman move his arm forward, before he could reach his coat buttons. It had proved impossible to coax Mikey into doing this, as he had forgotten the difference between forward and backward, and was, moreover, suspicious about being dislocated. They had fallen over in the course of the ensuing struggle, breaking the rod and loosening Vincent's wooden leg. At this stage Vincent had grown silent. He had worked with grim determination, concentrating on his buttons, a grimness which seemed to have unnerved Mikey so much that he bleated every time they rolled. Both of them had been aware—it was one of the things which Mr. White was inclined to explain to people—that the only part of the body which could not be touched with the right hand was the right elbow. Both had seemed determined to achieve the feat.

When the postman finally got out of his coat to freedom, he had picked Mikey up, arranged him in a suitable position, and hit his nose. Mikey had given a piercing cry and had sat down on the postman's spectacles, which had come off long before. Then, seeing that he was going to be picked up and punched again, he had scrambled to his feet as quickly as possible and taken to his heels, with the postman's coat still hooked to his back and the reel screaming as he went. The postman also had given out a piercing cry—for his reel—and, seizing the broken rod, had made a desperate effort to play Mikey like a salmon. Then, fearing for his line, which was practically all that remained to him, he had begun running after Mikey with the rod in his hand, in order to take the strain off the reel.

They had run like this for two fields, like royalty and train bearer at a rather hasty coronation, but Mikey had possessed two legs and no interest in the line. Also he had been urged forward by the postman's yells, not realizing that he had been forgiven, or that the postman was yelling for him to stop and save the reel. He had had the man bet, as he explained later, when they reached the thorny wire Back of Kelly's. The rod, and the postman, had become entangled in the wired gap; the line had extended itself, stretched, hummed, and snapped in the middle; Mikey, liberated at last, had sped away for the Avenue; and the heartbroken Vincent had been left to wind up the remains of his tackle.

Safe in the Burkestown Avenue, Mikey had paused for a brief moment to remove his two coats, like a medieval beaver biting off its testicles to evade pursuit, and had left them both on the white gate for the postman to find, as there was no time to struggle with the hooks.

He had reached home at last, still clutching his shattered twig, and it was from a combination of all these experiences that he was weeping in the soup plate.

Some of Mikey's tears were for the art of combining. Whether it was the attempted explanation, or the shocks which followed it, he was aware that the power had oozed out of him. He could no longer erect the twig.

Mr. White promised to spend all Sunday teaching him again.

When Sunday came, however, Mikey made no reference to the subject, and it was allowed to drop. The only art which he had ever learned had proved to be dangerous, so Mikey decided to be content with himself as he was in future.

CHAPTER XI

Before the uprights of the hay barn had been sawed off at the point A, mentioned some time ago, there had been a discussion on the proportions of the Ark, which had ended by their being cut at the point B after all. This not only saved the bother of cutting the side sheets to fit, for they could now be used entire, but it gave more cubic capacity to the Ark itself. The more Mr. White realized what a lot of things would need to be taken, the more he was anxious to have the Ark as deep as possible. He said that they would prevent her from riding too high by ballasting her with all the metal objects, like the horse roller, and even, if necessary, with a binder taken to bits—though he felt doubtful about being able to reassemble the mechanism which tied the knot— and that they would need a great deal of water for forty days, in tar barrels—when one considered the needs of the animals as well as of themselves—so it was best to increase both space and ballast. He said that he would make her not only watertight but airtight, if he died in the attempt, and that she could then lie in the Flood like a corked bottle three-quarters full of water, and they would have all the more materials for the new world.

The spare ends of the uprights had been used for the keel. Consequently there were no girders left for completing the frame of the Ark. She was, by now, like an inverted table with its legs in the air—only the actual lid of the table was trough-shaped, and there were eight legs. The feet, now uppermost, of these eight legs had to be joined together to complete the frame, and there was nothing with which to join them.

It had originally been intended to join them with lengths of two-by-two or of three-by-three, from the store of wood in the garage. But there were three objections to this. First, if the wood had to be bored for boltholes it would be weakened. Next, they were not sure how well the wood would marry with the metal, under the strains of rough weather. Lastly, as Mr. White pointed out, there would be plenty of wood available in the new world, but not necessarily any worked metal. The more assorted metal there was in the Ark itself, the better.

He and Pat Geraghty went to Cashelmor in the dray, and spent the day tacking from one merchant's to another, in search of girders. As all the merchants were grocers, and as all the grocers were publicans, the two shoppers grew merry and had a religious discussion on the way home.

Contrary to vulgar ideas about religion in the environs of Burkestown, this did not result in bloodshed. The reason was that Mr. White was so happy that he became a strong supporter of the Pope, out of compliment to Geraghty, and Geraghty, who had to stand up for Henry VIII, was not in possession of his facts. The latter was, moreover, mysteriously softened by his liquor instead of being exasperated by it. So they began singing instead— the pony could be relied upon to bring them safe— and Mr. White sang what he believed to be "Fill Every Glass," while Geraghty sang a kind of recitative about Parnell—or it may have been about

Napper Tandy. They had some difficulty in finding a song which they could sing together, but ended by hitting on *"Adeste Fideles,"* which they rendered all the way up the Burkestown avenue.

Mr. White kept Mrs. O'Callaghan and Mikey out of bed until three-thirty in the morning, explaining to them that Adrian IV was not an English pope and that Mr. De Valera was the most ill-educated man he had ever heard of, because he derived his faint ideas of history out of a book of balderdash by A. M. Sullivan. (Mrs. O'Callaghan never showed any restiveness when these things happened—indeed, she enjoyed them, for they were a change. She agreed thoroughly with Mr. White about that ould Dev. She said, Well now, Mr. White ought to thank God for his head.)

The interesting part of the business came when they started sorting out their purchases two days later. Mr. White had bought a perambulator, a kaleidoscope—what it was doing in Cashelmor, nobody knew—a goldfish, a saffron kilt, and half a dozen secondhand carpets from a sale. Fortunately they had also bought 150 feet of iron girder, L-shaped in section, like the frame of an iron bed and not much stronger. It was all they could get, and it would have to do.

Mr. White had invented a principle, since his conjuring days, that he would never drink at home. Consequently, on his twice-yearly visits to Cashelmor, he was apt to come back with unusual purchases, and as, on these days, he could generally be persuaded to pay his bills twice, he was a popular figure among the merchants of the town.

The L-shaped girders were used to join the table feet with bolts at each end, the joins being as follows:

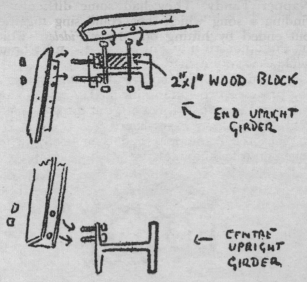

2"x1" WOOD BLOCK

↖ END UPRIGHT
    GIRDER

← CENTRAL
   UPRIGHT
   GIRDER

There were two bits in the tool cupboard which were suitable for boring metal, but unfortunately there was only the carpenter's brace. They adapted this for boring the girders by cutting the knob of the brace to a square, and by making a corresponding square to receive it under a six-foot plank, the latter square being like a small picture frame, into which the knob fitted. Then they put one end

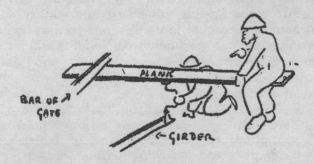

BAR OF ↗
GATE

PLANK

← GIRDER

of the plank under the bar of a gate or under anything else that was handy and Mr. White sat on the other end, to put pressure on the brace, while Geraghty turned it.

It was tedious work boring the strong girders by this process, as the bit was inclined to wander until it had made a road for itself, but the corrugated sheets bored more easily later.

When the framework had been finally bolted together, it looked like this:

picture up-side-down!

Meanwhile, the lists continued in the evenings, and there were a few external complications, due to the reactions of the neighbors. Pat Geraghty had at first talked freely of the Ark to everybody he met; Philomena had overheard enough of the lists to be able to corroborate his story; and the Ark itself was beginning to take shape. The anonymous letters, which were usual in matters of agriculture round Cashelmor, began to arrive before anything else. The first one—which was written by Geraghty himself, whose relations with his master were gradually worsening, as will have to be explained later—said clearly:

Kind Sir

We are eight tennents in Cashelmor we are informed that you are giving Potion of Mikey O'Callaghan's barn to James Heraghty and Pat Donohue and wife for creating mischief the have a slattet house

But he dont want to Pay the Rint and the Rates of It to the man who gave it to him get a Place for us eight tennents some eigher where our cattle cannot Pass Back or over But they have the hunted with dog if you are going to give him Possion of mikey O'Callaghans barn we will see to furder incuries so Please watch your self

yours truley eight
tennents
Cashelmor

The second said:

mister Whyte
You have me hous took doun on me amost reddy But if you Do not imeditly you will Catc it

A FRIEND

This one was from Mikey. Mrs. O'Callaghan found out by the handwriting and was angry with him. She said that if Mr. White wanted to take down the barn it was not for a person with a head like Mikey's to interfere.

The third letter said:

Your Honr
We know what You are at sir an to Wipe out if necery wit Blood eny furder goings On to the insult of our Relegion So beleive us yours affecly

a Christan

This was from Philomena's twenty-three brothers and sisters.

The fourth said:

Mr Whyte Esq.

I have me hay Bt. of Mikey O'Callaghan this 23 yeers an Free passage By slane meadow when the cow straid but now You are Pulling it down widout a Though for Poor men an Nieghbours like a Vandle which is as Some especcid for wance a shoneen allways but Justice Shall Prevail

a Ribel

Nobody ever found out who wrote this, for it can scarcely have been Mrs. O'Callaghan. Perhaps it was Tommy Plunkett.

Apart from the literary moves, there was little serious reaction to the Ark for the time being. There was a certain amount of booing, and stones were thrown at the vessel during the night; but, as it was not combustible, there was no damage.

Booing was a custom applied by local consent to widows who married again. It was done by knocking the bottom out of a glass bottle and hooting through it, outside the bridal chamber, at night. The noise produced was not unlike the note of a horn. With this, and the clang of stones rattling on galvanized iron, and the incessant barking of Diamond or Tiny, rest was disturbed at Burkestown for a few nights.

The reason why the Ark was received with such tolerance was twofold. In the first place, almost everything was received with tolerance round Burkestown, on account of the atmosphere. The rain clouds which swept in from the southwest, bearing the leaden mass of moisture accumulated in three thousand miles of the Atlantic, oppressed the aborigines with such a weight that it was sufficiently difficult to attend to their own concerns, without attending to the troubles of other people. The second reason was, that all but the wildest hotheads and agitators had realized, after short reflection, how easy it would be to destroy the O'Callaghan Ark later on. Let us, said they, make what we can out of it in the first place. We can always roast Mr. White to death, or bury him alive in a pit full of thorns, when there is no further financial return to be anticipated.

Large numbers of neighbors began to present themselves at the house, offering various pairs of animals for the venture. Wren boys, accustomed to the capture of live birds by pursuing them until too exhausted to proceed further, in order to gratify St. Stephen, brought not only wrens, but also blackbirds, thrushes, robins, and other defenseless fauna, which they were prepared to sell for a song, so long as the song were not provided by the birds. Various "herds" offered the sheep, calves, and other livestock owned by their employers. Twenty-seven goats and thirteen donkeys were on the market, mostly of the masculine gender. Vendors of turf, brass bedsteads, pianos, broken bicycle frames, knitting machines with essential ports missing, phonograph horns, senile race horses, eggs, photographs of the penultimate pope, standing trees, empty bottles, odd pairs of boots, and superannuated threshing machines thronged the approaches, refusing to see anybody but Mr. White. They intimidated him by calling him Y'r Honor, a phrase which was never used except as a preliminary to attrition. They screamed with rage when he bought anything, hoping to extract three times its value instead of twice.

The farmers of the neighborhood, who usually exchanged a single round of visits at Christmas and left it at that, began calling every evening with their wives, in order to sit round the damp drawing room on hard chairs, while they waited for something to be said. They were too polite to make inquiries.

Father Byrne did not call. It was felt at this period that Mr. White, being an Englishman, had probably laid a trap for the Catholic Church, and it would be safer not to fall into it.

It became impossible to make lists in the evening, owing to the interruptions, so the time for lists was transferred to the morning, while Mikey was separating or churning.

A bad spell of weather destroyed the remains of the harvest.

Tommy Plunkett and the maid Philomena gave notice, but there was nothing unusual in this. Mikey and Mrs. O'Callaghan had long come to a compromise in their technique for running the farm, by which the blame for all disasters, when finally refused by both of them, was to be laid upon the hired labor. The result was that few employees remained for more than three months.

A feature of the disasters which prevailed at Burkestown, by the way, was that Mrs. O'Callaghan and Mikey were able to increase them by co-operation. Just as M. and Mme. Curie worked together toward the discovery of radium, each mind striking fire from the other's, so Mr. and Mrs. O'Callaghan, working together, contrived to make confusion worse confounded. For instance, if Mrs. O'Callaghan had suddenly decided to whitewash the kitchen range, she was sure to mix the lime in one of the enamel cream basins, and to leave it in the dairy. Alone, she could not have gone much further. It needed Mikey to come in at this point, to pour the whitewash into the week's collection of cream, and to churn the mixture all morning. Or, if Mikey had suddenly decided to poison rats in the oat loft, he could be relied upon to leave the packet of phosphorus on the kitchen sideboard with the mustard; but it needed Mrs. O'Callaghan to find it, and to give a good feed of it to the collie dog, under the impression that it was bloater paste. Mrs. O'Callaghan, working alone, could put Mr. White's Sunday vest into the oven to air, start doing something else, and forget it until it was baked to a cinder; she could go further, and could throw the remains of the vest, with several pieces of broken glass, into one of the milk buckets. But it needed Mikey to come then, to milk the cows into the bucket, without troubling to clean it, and then to pass the solution through the separator until the latter was jammed.

The effect of these surprises was that the O'Callaghans seemed to be laying traps for each other.

Another effect was to increase the effort needed in distributing blame. The blame for simple disasters could be thrown from one to the other with the speed of thought. In compound disasters, achieved by co-operation, the strain became heavier. Mrs. O'Callaghan had to say that the separator was broken because Mikey did not clean the buckets, to which Mikey had to reply that it was broken because Mrs. O'Callaghan put vests and glass in them, and Mrs. O'Callaghan had to counter by saying that it wasn't her fault because she could not bake in a cold oven so that Mr. White's vest had to be roasted in order to provide Mikey with new bread and she a slave, and separating and bread and vests and whitewash and slaves and cream and blame and everything else would become involved in a traffic jam, much like the jam in the separator, from which it was difficult to find an exit, particularly as Mrs. O'Callaghan's views on traffic control were partial to the Roundabout.

Since neither of them cared for thinking about

the future or about the things which might need
to be done in the coming year, preferring to mull
over the bills which were two years out of date
and to blame each other for something which
went wrong with the churn in 1936, this co-
operation in confusion was a blessing to both. It
gave them something to be muddled with, and it
involved their speculations.

Mikey had a private defense, which consisted in
saying, "Hwrrk?" When he had failed to notice
that a cow was going to calve, with the result that
the calf or cow or both had died in childbirth;
when he had purposely overlooked the ploughing
quota and been caught by some itinerant inspector;
when he had delayed sending the sugar beet until
the factory was closed, after a series of printed
warnings; when he had failed to feed the farm
dogs for three days, or left five cows to die of
starvation in one winter, to save the trouble of
giving them hay, or allowed the sheep to get so
full of summer maggots that they were eaten in
half, somebody, generally Mr. White, would set an
inquiry on foot. It was then that Mikey said,
"Hwrrk?" while he thought up a *tu quoque*.

CHAPTER
XII

M r. White changed hands on the churn with-out interrupting himself.

"Put down medicine," he said.

Mrs. O'Callaghan wrote "Medecen" in her copy-book and waited for further instructions.

"We shall have to take morphia and perhaps a pair of dental forceps and some sulfanilamide or other and a first-aid box and some Carter's Little Liver Pills—perhaps we could manage to grow castor oil from seeds—and we must find out what is best for rheumatism. I think it is phenyl quino-line and carboxylic acid. So far as I can see, the whole science of medicine is summed up in aperi-ents, anesthetics, bonesetting, and three or four genuine remedies like insulin. I wonder if I could learn to vaccinate? We must make our own splints."

Ker-lump, ker-lump, ker-lump: The churn saved Mrs. O'Callaghan from having to spell these.

"As for the hayseed and all that," said Mr. White, going off at a tangent, "we shall have to stow it in tea chests, to prevent it from shifting. Grain is a dangerous cargo if you leave it loose."

Mrs. O'Callaghan's favorite medicine was aspi-rin. She wrote it down guiltily, without instruc-tions, and also wrote "Red Flanil."

"How strange it is," observed Mr. White, peep-ing in at the window to see if the butter had come yet, "to be the arbiters of a future world. For instance, we have it in our own hands to decide whether the future is to be teetotal or not. If we take a still, we shall carry the secret of fermented liquor for our children. Shall we take a still?"

"Whatever you like, Mr. White."

"The knowledge of distillation will be in the *Encyclopædia Britannica,* for a future generation to read about if it likes, so ours is really an academic question. I don't propose to start censoring the *Encyclopædia.* We could tear out the pages devoted to liquor, explosives, harmful drugs, poisons, and so on, but it would be a difficult job to censor the whole work efficiently, and I am not sure whether censorship is ever morally defensible. What is, is. I am opposed to suppressing any form of truth, however dangerous.

"What we will do is this: We will take the *Encyclopædia,* but we will not take a still. After all, there are other things asking for space which are more urgent. Then, when the new world has settled down, the future can make up its own mind about constructing stills.

"And the question of explosives. Shall we take my two shotguns or not? No doubt there will be large numbers of birds trying to perch on the Ark, during her voyage, and we could add to our precarious provisions by shooting these. On the other hand, guns and cartridges are more bulky and weighty than people suppose. A cartridge takes up quite as much space as the meat on a teal. Besides, if we do not take the guns, there will be no chance of our shooting each other in a moment of passion. I myself am thoroughly sick of Friar Bacon's invention, and I am in favor of not taking the guns, even if it means a slight inconvenience. Besides, if our descendents insist on reviving gunpowder, it is all there for them in the

Encyclopædia. Let us, at least, set them a humane example so far as we can."

"We could take some holy water."

"A whole barrel of it, if you like, so long as there is no objection to drinking it. We will ask Father Byrne to bless the barrels."

"Can we take the Infant of Prague?"

Mr. White was the kindest of men. He disapproved of the Infant of Prague almost as much as he disapproved of Titsy, but he felt, on principle, that people ought to be allowed to be happy in their own way. After all, he was taking wind machines and dental forceps to amuse himself.

"You can pack a tea chest with your own things, Mrs. O'Callaghan, and so can Mikey. I mean, things which are not on the lists. Put the Infant of Prague in yours. I suppose Mikey will fill his chest with tobacco, if he can get enough money to buy it. By the way, have you fixed to auction the farm?"

"We didn' exacly fix it."

A dreadful, instantaneous, illuminating suspicion flashed across his mind like lightning, causing him to stop the churn.

"Who is to do the auction?"

"We didn' exacly . . ."

"Are you going to sell it?"

"I don't think Mikey wants to sell it, because he had it from his Anty."

"Good God," cried Mr. White, churning and stopping and churning again and stopping for good, "what does it matter whether Mikey had the farm from his aunt? When it has been swept away by the Flood, he won't have had it from anybody."

"But his Ant lef it him."

"I don't care if it was left him by his grandmother. The point is that we have a farm at present, which we can sell, and as soon as the flood comes we shan't have a farm at all, and can't sell it. We need the money."

"But suppose there doesn't be a Flood?"

As usual, he made the fatal mistake of trying to explain from the beginning. It was fatal because, the further back he started, the more ground he had to cover, and consequently the more opportunity there was for Mrs. O'Callaghan to pursue her assorted hares, such as Ants, stomachs, Divine Omnipotence, prophecy, and the Holy Will of God. She had an effective, if unconscious, technique for argument. Her lines of defense were subtle, and she never relied on one of them by itself. It was more by the labyrinth, by the multiplicity of outworks, that she gained her defensive victories.

First of all, she used to erect a sham bastion, a wall, as it were, made of lath and cardboard, with which to "amuse" her adversary, as the military people put it. Mr. White, like the bull in Spain, always consumed enormous energies against this cloak, which she waved before him, without achieving anything, and, indeed, without being clear in his mind about what he was trying to do. In the present case, the deception was, of course, the Ant. Mrs. O'Callaghan did not seriously believe in Mikey's Ant, but she relied on her to consume as much as possible of Mr. White's preliminary momentum. When the Ant was exhausted—and she was of no importance to Mrs. O'Callaghan, so that she could finally be yielded without regret—the successive earthworks, smoke screens, chevaux-de-frise, re-entrant angles, and so forth, of an elastic defense in depth, were for the first time spread out before the invader—already weakened by his efforts against the Ant.

Since this is the story of an Ark, it might be fair

to say that Mr. White was the elephant, Mrs. O'Callaghan the kangaroo.

"If," said he, "there was not going to be a Flood, why did the Archangel say there was?"

"Perhaps she made a mistake."

"How can an Archangel make a mistake? An Archangel is God's messenger, isn't It? And God is omnipotent and omniscient and omnipresent and all the other things you tell me about, twice a week. If It is omniscient, how can It make a mistake?"

"But, Mr. White, we know that *everybody* makes mistakes, sometimes."

"What does omniscient mean?" he asked, with deadly calm.

"I can't just remember, not at the minute."

"It means to know everything."

"I knowed it meant something like that. But I forgot."

"Well, then, if It knows everything, how can It make mistakes?"

"We can't tell that, Mr. White. It does be the Holy . . ."

" . . . Will of God!" screamed Mr. White, seizing the churn handle and whirling it round like a dervish.

Mrs. O'Callaghan watched him sympathetically, and wrote down "Milk of Magnesia" (for when her stomach should be at her). The first round was plainly in her favor.

"If," said he, pausing exhausted, "if you are a Christian (as you pretend to be, though, God knows, I sometimes think, but, no, I won't start side issues), if, as I was saying, you are a Christian (and not a worshiper of Baal, or whoever it was the ancient Irish used to worship, I must look it up, though of course, among others, the goddess Dana), if, then, you are (or prefer to think you are) a

Christian (black cats excepted, for they were wor-
shiped by the Egyptians), and if you are not a
benighted cannibal bemused by the superstitions
of prehistory . . ."

He took the handle again with an absent look,
and began to churn peacefully, at the right speed.

"I never could understand," he observed, "what
objection there is to being a cannibal. To kill your
fellow men: that strikes me as being immoral. But,
once you have killed them, why not eat them? At
least it is putting them to a useful purpose, instead
of wasting them completely. . . ."

He peeped in, to search for butter.

"If, Mrs. O'Callaghan, you are a Christian, then
you are supposed to believe that God knows everything. If God knows everything, and says there
is going to be a Flood, then there is going to be a
Flood. Isn't that so?"

"Perhaps there will be a Flood somewhere else,
in Germany or one of thim places."

"If there is going to be a Flood in Germany,
why did the Archangel come here to tell us about
it?"

"Perhaps she wanted us to know."

"But why us, instead of the Germans? After all,
if the Flood was going to be in Germany, I suppose it would be more rational . . ."

He stopped hastily. He could see the Holy Will
of God looming ahead.

"Mrs. O'Callaghan, do you believe there is going
to be a Flood?"

"Yes," she said, beginning to sweat a bit.

"Do you believe that it was an Archangel?"

"Yes."

"And the Archangel told us to build an Ark?"

"Yes," said Mrs. O'Callaghan doubtfully.

"Well then, if the Archangel told us to build an
Ark because there is going to be a Flood, why not

sell the farm, which will be destroyed anyway, in order to help us build the Ark?"

"She did not tell us to sell it.'

"Yes, but She—It—told us to build the Ark. The rest was left to us. There is an *implication* that we should sell the farm, in the very fact that we were told to build the Ark."

"You said she didn' tell you to get married, Mr. White."

"That has nothing to do with it."

After a bit, he added: "The cases are not parallel."

Finally, being a fair-minded man, he stopped churning and went out to find Mikey.

CHAPTER XIII

Brownie had finished the glue; the swallows, for some weeks hawking over the sodden harvest, had taken themselves off to brighter climes; the booers had lost interest; even the anonymous letter writers, after a final communication about fishing tackle from the postman, who signed himself "Two Catholic Mothers," had subsided into lethargy. The Ark was well advanced.

There were a pair of blacksmiths within reach of Burkestown. From one of these, the shipwrights had ordered a gross of angle brackets in the usual shape.

From the other blacksmith they ordered a gross of brackets shaped like this:

These were the only fittings of the Ark not made on the premises, and the two smiths were employed in order to get the metal delivered quickly. Neither smith proved able to understand any form of drawing or description of the bracket needed, so two full-sized specimens had to be made from tin, and a piece of the required metal had to be enclosed with each order.

The brackets were intended to save the trouble of having to bore the upper horizontal girders for bolts, when fitting the galvanized sheets of the sides and roof (or deck).

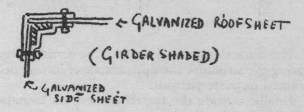

← GALVANIZED ROOFSHEET

(GIRDER SHADED)

← GALVANIZED SIDE SHEET

Owing to the fact that the galvanized sheets were fluted, these brackets could only be bolted in the trough of a flute. Consequently, the joins along the edges of the Ark were not watertight. Each edge had a gaping row of semicircular apertures:

But when the sides and deck had been bolted on—the sheeting being procured partly from the garage and partly from the original sides—then these gaps were hammered as flat as possible along the girders. It did not look tidy, and it was not waterproof, but it was a step in the right direction.

The secondhand carpets purchased during the carouse in Cashelmor were now cut into strips twelve inches wide, and were tarred. These strips were laid along the hammered edges, outside, so that half the strip lay on the deck and the other half hung down the side of the Ark.

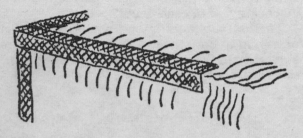

The same thing was done with the vertical edges, giving the structure the appearance of having been framed in passe partout.

Finally, outside the tarred carpets, an L-shaped gutter of galvanized iron was hammered down well to the tar and bolted tightly, with tarred washers round the bolts. These troughs or gutters were cut from the remaining sheets of the garage, by making perforations with the cold chisel, and were flattened into shape by hammering them on the sawed butt of a tree stump with the sledge. They were shaped like this:

They fitted over the carpet binding, or passe partout.

The Ark now had the appearance of having been framed, not with passe partout, but with gray metal, as it had been. It was externally complete, except for its entrances. They had decided, in the course of construction, not to leave the whole of one of the ends open—as had originally been intended, so that the beasts could be led in—but only to leave off three sheets from that end, which would provide a sufficient opening. Then, in the storm and stress of embarkation, it would be a matter of bolting on no more than three sheets, instead of having to complete the whole end. The other entrance was to be a trap door in the deck.

Before the trap door, and the interior fittings, were to be attempted, it was thought best to go round the exterior edges of the Ark with tar, cotton waste, cold chisel, and hammer. The tarred waste was hammered in with the edge of the chisel at any point which seemed doubtfully watertight. The waste itself was procured by Mr. White, who tore up most of Mrs. O'Callaghan's best sheets and all his own handkerchiefs.

While the caulking was going on, however, there came an alteration in the relations between the builders.

The trouble between Mr. White and Pat Geraghty was that the one was of Alpine while the other was of Mediterranean race. Geraghty, although insane to a scarcely noticeable extent, was in other respects a normal aborigine of Cashelmor. He had spent his life in the environs of Burkestown. All his neighbors had always been either thieves or swindlers or assassins. He, and they, believed, with the O'Callaghans, that the moon's changes changed the weather; that sunlight extinguished fires; that the best cure for whooping cough lay in passing the sufferer under the belly of a donkey; that there was a real and tangible fire in Hell, where Mr. White would be roasted, without being consumed, by a benevolent deity, for the rest of eternity; that it would rain if a curlew were heard; that Purgatory, where he himself would go, was also a place of actual fire, but not eternal; that "frost brings rain"—a not unnatural belief, when one reflects that, in winter, if it is not dry and frosty it is pretty well sure to be wet and rainy; that wagtails were birds of death, like the chaladrius; that three candles in one ¡room would bring a death before the end of the year; that women must not cut men's hair; that there was a "stray sod" near Burkestown and that, if the traveler stepped on it, he would lose his way for the rest of the night unless he had the presence of mind to turn his waistcoat back to front; that a weasel should be spat upon when met; that the banshee sounded a little like an amorous cat; and that Ireland was the land of Saints and Scholars, whose saintly and scholarly activities had only been handicapped by the barbarous interference of English cannibals like Mr. White. All these things, and a great many more, were believed by Pat as simply as it is believed in other places that the milkman will call in the morning. Since scarcely any of them were believed by his master, there was, of course, a barrier between them.

It was not so much what Geraghty believed, however, as what he was accustomed to understand by his environment, that caused the trouble. So far as his experience went, the main objective of human beings was to take advantage of one another. In recognizing this, indeed, he and his neighbors offered perhaps their best claim to possessing greater perspicuity than their oppressors across the water.

He was now, for external reasons, beginning to worry about being employed by a venomous Englishman. "Four things not to trust," said the Cashelmor proverb: "a dog's tooth, a horse's hoof, a cow's horn, and an Englishman's laugh." It was beginning to seem to Geraghty that he was in a dangerous situation.

On top of this, there was the Ark.

In the beginning, he had enjoyed building the thing, in his innocence, just as he enjoyed working with Mr. White, who humored him so carefully. Then there had come the booing, and other local reactions, which had awakened him, for the first time, to the nature of his occupation.

The poor man wanted to know what the devil Mr. White was getting at.

He had worked, had even enjoyed working, all this time; he had kept a Burkestown eye upon his master, waiting to see through the latter's tricks and to thwart the inevitable attempt to do the employee down. Yet no attempt had been made; no trick had been identified. It was enough to give any Gael the brain fever.

Pat Geraghty had lately reviewed the position as carefully as possible, since the booing and since some other developments throughout Kildare, which will have to be explained later, and he had taken care not to give his employer credit for being altruistic, affectionate, simple, truthful, or for having any of the supposed virtues in which Cashelmor did not believe. The only construction which he could place upon the position—since his master was obviously cheating him somehow or other, even if he could not see how, and since the two qualities in which all Gaels did believe were tireless cunning and malevolence—was that the Ark was being built *in order to make a fool of him.*

This, incidentally, was the only doom that was dreaded throughout the land. It was possible, indeed it had been usual, to flog the Gael, to ruin him, to starve him, to transport him, to paint him with tar and set him alight, to trample on his neck, or to hang him in large quantities over your shoulder. He had rather liked it. But if you wrote a satire upon him, if you made him look a fool, he immediately curled up and died.

Naturally, therefore, Pat had sworn to be revenged.

Nor had he to seek vengeance only for the cruel insult of the Ark. There was, he had begun to realize, the matter of the mischief created by James Geraghty and Pat Donohue and wife over the slattit house, which he had lucidly explained in his anonymous letter, and there also remained outstanding the complicated injustice, which, as he at last saw clearly, could only have been engineered by Mr. White, of the deaf and dumb sister, and the two and one-half pairs of stockings, and the wedge.

In short, Mr. White had paid him for two years because he did not believe him to be guilty about the wedge, which was sufficient reason to believe that Mr. White had himself planted it on him; he had done his best to be a helpful employer, which was sufficient reason for Geraghty to suppose that he had been swindled all round; and he had realized that the only local workman clever enough to help with the Ark was Geraghty, which was sufficient reason for Geraghty to believe that the Ark was being built on purpose to make a fool of him.

Finally, of course, one has to remember that it is insufferable to have a master, and doubly insufferable if one happens to be afflicted with delusions of grandeur.

This was the side of the matter which confused Pat. It was the part of the confusion which arose from Mr. White's habit of telling the truth. The other side of the matter, which confused Mr. White, arose from his own habit of believing what he was told. The latter, in fact, was generally at a double remove from the reality of his surroundings, because everything he said was instinctively disbelieved by his hearers—which confused them, since what he said was true—and everything they said was instinctively believed by Mr. White—which confused him, since what they said was not true. In the upshot he was usually left to forge ahead through a phantom world of his own: a kind of Flying Dutchman of the intellect, voyaging through strange seas of thought alone.

For Geraghty, who was nothing if not a product of Cashelmor, had immediately reacted to his own decision of being signally revenged upon his persecutor by behaving as if he now loved him better than his life. He had begun telling Mr. White, with every other breath, that he was the kindest gintleman he had ivver mit.

Mr. White, who personally saw no reason to doubt this, told Mrs. O'Callaghan that the great virtue of the Irish was their capacity for gratitude: that, and hospitality. And simplicity, he added.

Mrs. O'Callaghan looked puzzled.

Pat's first attempts to get justice had been ineffectual. He had written several new letters, signing himself I.R.A., with a picture of a bloody dagger in red ink. His insensitive correspondent, who had frequently sent such letters himself at his preparatory school, had pasted these in a scrapbook with stupid pleasure. Pat had then tried to poison Brownie, offering her a few moldy bones drenched with strychnine; but, as Brownie seldom ate anything except Mr. White's dinner, the gentle effort had met with no success. The next thing had been to write to the I.R.A. themselves, and also to Father Byrne, denouncing his oppressor to the one as a Russian spy and to the other as a Mormon. The I.R.A. had been too busy smuggling the type of weapon suitable for assassinations to bother their heads with an eccentric author, and Father Byrne did not at that time care if Mr. White were a Manichee, so long as he laid no plots against the vested interests of the mother of churches.

In the end, there had been nothing for it but the national solution. Pat Geraghty had decided, for the honor of Ireland, to shoot Mr. White as dead as mutton, from behind a hedge.

CHAPTER
XIV

On the night of his murder, our hero was in hot pursuit of one of his red herrings. Possibly he needed mental relaxation from the problems of the Ark; but in any case he was a convinced follower of herrings, whose interests seldom required a particular excuse. He had, for instance, learned to fly an airplane in the days of Moths, only to stop flying as soon as he had a license to do so; had trained all the European hawks, even owning a gyrfalcon for a fortnight, only to give them their liberty as soon as they were trained; had found out, and forgot, how to describe an achievement of arms correctly; had written a book about Admiral Byng which nobody could publish, because it was mainly about "lasking" and about various Admiralty instructions which nobody could understand any better than poor Byng; had been arrested, by mistake, and then released, for trying to assassinate Mussolini; had spent two years making extraordinary pictures in oils, bearing glass eyes stuck to them with putty, only to destroy them all; had been mistaken for St. Patrick by an archbishop during a pilgrimage, only to become a freethinker; had translated three pages from a twelfth-century bestiary, but grown tired of it; had accepted the mastership of a pack of harriers, which turned out not to belong to the committee;

had tried to learn Irish, in which language he could still conduct such advanced conversations as Konus Thaw Thu? Thaw May GoMoy, Gorrer Mealy Moy Agot; and had once caused his appendix to be removed, for fear that he might at some future date be struck with appendicitis. He had, however, never been tattooed.

Mr. White, then, had suddenly informed Mrs. O'Callaghan that there were three things which everybody ought to know about themselves. They ought to know the blood group to which they belonged, the peculiarities of their fingerprints, and their own cephalic index.

No sooner said than done. Rushing upstairs to the playroom on the first crest of enthusiasm, he had unearthed a long forgotten tube of printing ink, with which he had been accustomed to make linocuts, and had smeared Mrs. O'Callaghan and himself and Mikey with a liberal coating, in order to take the fingerprints. Not possessing the necessary apparatus for testing the blood group, he had hurried back to make himself a pair of calipers, at any rate, for the cephalic index.

He had made the calipers out of plywood, cutting arms for them like the arms of a wooden compass used on blackboards, and bolting them together with a copper rivet.

Then, with a few minutes to spare before the nine-o'clock news bulletin from the B.B.C., he had hastened down to the kitchen, to measure Mikey and Mrs. O'Callaghan. Mikey's index had proved to be sixty, Mrs. O'Callaghan's sixty-two, and Mr. White had reached the dining-room wireless in high fettle, switching on the electric light as he went, just in time to hear the news.

Geraghty had been waiting outside the window. He was hiding in what Mrs. O'Callaghan called the rosy-dendrums, a prey to superstitious fear.

He had stolen Mr. White's B.S.A. magnum, which the latter had once used for shooting wild geese, before he became an opponent of blood sports, and had obtained seven Irish-made cartridges in Cashelmor, which had no maker's name printed on them. Only that morning he had made his last attempt to be revenged upon his master, without actually murdering him, by slashing the motor tires in the garage with a scythe. In order to be in character as an English cannibal, Mr. White ought to have evicted his employee forthwith, or to have afflicted him with a famine, or to have caused him to emigrate, or at least he ought to have handed him over to the Garda Siochana. Instead, he had preserved an incomprehensible silence on the subject. This accounted for the superstitious fear now torturing his assassin, who did not know that Mr. White, who seldom noticed his motor any longer, was unaware that the tires had been assaulted.

Indeed, there was much for Pat to dread. There were the red bottles which made people vomit, the bushy beard, the mystery of the Ark, the familiar spirit (Brownie), the unbelievable cunning by which the Saxon overreached people without even letting them know that they had been overreached, the diabolic skill with which he told lies which nobody could detect, the satanic interest in ants and other creatures which only existed to be stamped upon by rational persons, and, above all, there was the appearance of Mr. White himself—shaggy, enthusiastic, earnest, energetic, childishly veracious: obviously a devilish pose.

The victim switched on the wireless and sat down in a Nelson chair, clutching the calipers.

The bright pink lampshade outlined his whiskers, wild and fibrous; the noble brow leaned forward intelligently, with something of a leonine expression, as the wireless roared out its usual list of atrocities—which surged and howled against the calm cliff of its listener's world-rambling mind. Mr. White, with his calipers and silent face, voyaging . . .

When Pat came to cover the cliff-forehead with the B.S.A., at a range of about eight yards, his bowels were suddenly pierced with pity. He remembered the kindnesses which his master had shown to him. It seemed almost indecent to shoot an unsuspecting, defenseless, and benevolent person from behind a hedge. The foreign thought made Pat feel ashamed of himself, but there it was. He almost had a mind to let the Englishman live.

The assassinee, meanwhile, was only partly interested in the fall of empires. So many had fallen, so much news of bloodshed had poured out of the atmosphere during his lifetime, that his sympathies had become dulled in this respect. The question of the cephalic index, on the other hand, was new. In spite of the bulletin, he began to measure his skull.

Pat Geraghty watched in horror. His pity forgotten, his knees knocking together and the gun barrel revolving round the forehead in circles, he viewed the cabalistic motions dumbly. It was, he saw, in a flash of intuition, just as all the neighbors had always suspected. Mr. White was putting on his horns.

The calipers were about fourteen inches long, bifurcated like a draftsman's compass. It was true that Mr. White was putting them on upside down, but he could be relied upon to do that. Satan himself, the figure in the penny catechism, robing for some aerial journey to who knew what Sabbath in the bogs of Cashelmor, sat outlined in the full glare of the electric light—but curiously pitiful and private, as people are when they pursue their simple interests in the belief that they are unobserved.

Mr. White stood up and switched off the wireless. He sat down again, searching for a pencil, produced the foot rule from his pocket, measured the distance between the points of his horns, and made a note. Then he clapped them to his head in another position, measured, and noted. Leaning forward over the shining table, he began to divide 98 by 123—his unit was the sixteenth of an inch—and to multiply by 100. Ha, said he to himself, I am just within the bounds of being brachycephalic, and I am also melanochrous though my eyes are blue. . . .

It was too much for Geraghty's never powerful brains. The act of writing—a black art—put the lid on it. He leveled the magnum with trembling fingers, hung heavily on the aim—which would certainly have made him poke, if he had been shooting partridges—and pressed the trigger.

It was lucky for the Ark that they were Irish cartridges.

Mr. White, hearing the click, looked up and peered through the indigo window. Then, interested but not satisfied, he went round to the hall door and gazed out.

Pat was still trying the same trigger, too horrified to try the other cartridge, which might, with luck, have worked.

"Is anybody there?"

The figure in the rosy-dendrums gave a sob.

"Oh, it is you, Pat, is it? Have you been shooting? Come in and have a drink."

The magician led his captive into the dining room, identified the magnum with faint disapproval, but was too interested in brachycephalism to follow the matter up, and poured out a glass of whisky, talking merrily.

Geraghty listened in a maze. It was about the
Fir Bolg and the Tuatha De Danaan and whether
your hair was yellow and if your skull was long or
round. He was made to sit in the chair which the
witch doctor had just vacated; he was given whisky,
which he drank like a dying fish; the horns were
affixed to his own head; he was beyond speech or
understanding.

When Mr. White finally let him out, smiling
genially, clapping him on the back, and promising
to clean the gun himself, Pat darted away into the
shrubbery like a throbbing bird escaped from human hands. He lay there perdu, gasping, repeat-
ing the general confession. When he had recovered
a little, he glanced back into the lighted window.

The Saxon had resumed his seat. Smiling away
with fiendish calm, his head turned slightly toward
the wall between himself and his assassin, and
with the light behind him, he was holding his
two hands together, the elbows resting on the
arms of the chair. As Geraghty watched, one of
the fingers came out, then two. They agitated
themselves. The hands writhed in convulsive passes,
turned about on their axis, wriggled out palm
upward, and began to flap their thumbs. The little
finger hooked itself with indescribable menace.
Finally the index extended with awful delibera-
tion, straight at its victim's heart.

The latter ran for his life.

Howling and blubbering to Almighty God,
Blessed Mary Ever Virgin, Blessed Michael the
Archangel, Blessed John Baptist, the Holy Apos-
tles Peter and Paul, and all the Saints, and you
Father, he vanished into the night.

Mr. White, who was childishly making shadow
animals on the wall, with his hands, shifted round
to get a better profile. He was good at rabbits—
which anybody could do—and he could also man-

age crocodiles with their mouths open, without much difficulty. He could do a turkey gobbler by using both hands, an art which one needed to learn. The trouble, he thought, is to get the eye to remain motionless while you make it gobble.

CHAPTER
XV

The second shipwright never returned to work, so that our hero was left to complete the furnishings by himself. He was distressed by the inexplicable absence of his protégé, and sent down several messages to the deaf and dumb sister, asking if there was anything that he could do. All answers stated that Pat was suffering from double pneumonia in both ankles, and would be back at work tomorrow. Also, on the front doorstep, running the gauntlet of the bees in the hall fanlight, there appeared two and a half pairs of stockings and a wedge.

The Ark was complete except for its interior. What remained to be done was not beyond the power of one workman.

The first thing was to stow the heavy ballast in the trough of the inverted roof: ballast which consisted of the farm machinery taken to pieces, plow, harrows, rake, grubber, etc., and of the smithing tools, with a stock of iron rods; in fact, of everything heavy, not needed on voyage, and not likely to be spoiled by damp. There would probably be some bilge in this compartment, Mr. White explained, so it was only the sturdy and less perishable metal objects which could be packed there.

At this stage, he became excited about a binder. He said that there was room for one, if dismantled, that it would be of priceless value to them, and that he was prepared to learn how to put it together again, if he died in the attempt. But it was a question of twine.

"We cannot take enough twine to keep the machine in action for more than a year or two," said he, "because there is no room, and I do not know how to make a twine that would stand up to it, I mean in the New World." He had begun to think of the New World in capitals, like stout Cortes. "Even," he continued, "if we were to take enough twine for ten years, which is all that we could possibly stow, by throwing out other necessaries, it would still be an unprofitable investment. We have to plan," said he to Mrs. O'Callaghan, pointing his pencil at her, "for *posterity*. Ten years is of no importance compared with the Future, and we must not selfishly consider our temporary convenience, at the expense of the remote objective."

"Just what you think, Mr. White," said Mrs. O'Callaghan politely.

"Then we will reap," he said, "with scythes. If our children want a binder, they will just have to make one for themselves, out of the *Encyclopædia Britannica*. By the way, I must fit the pump so that it goes down to the bottom of the bilge, and keeps everything as dry as it can."

"Mr. White," said Mrs. O'Callaghan plaintively, as though reasoning with him about some unusually difficult object which he had asked her to put on the shopping list, "you can't ask *me* to have them, you know."

"No."

"Childer . . ."

"I know all about that, Mrs. O'Callaghan. *We must leave them to the Holy Will of God.*"

"But God," said Mrs. O'Callaghan, acknowledging the hit with a simpler, "doesn't be able to do anything which is not *possible*, Mr. White."

"*Everything*," said Mr. White piously, "*is possible to God.*"

This left him free to return to the subject of reaping, which was not exhausted by a first decision to use scythes.

"If we took a binder after all," said he, "I am sure that I could take off the part which ties the knot, in one piece. It would not use up more space than a bucket, and we could keep it like that. Of course, what we really ought to take is a combine harvester, if there were any hope of getting one in this accursed country, but there is not. We should need a king's ransom for that." Here Mr. White looked accusingly at Mrs. O'Callaghan, who still refused to sell the farm.

It was not that she actually refused to do so; indeed, she frequently consented; but the fact was that she took no steps. Mikey's Ant had been swept away in numerous engagements, and there had been a terrific pincer movement on the subject of the infallibility of Archangels, which had naturally become involved with the infallibility of the Pope. Here Mrs. O'Callaghan was on strong ground, for she pointed out, with rigid logic, that the Archangel Michael was not the Pope.

"If," said Mr. White bitterly, "we had a bit more money, we could try to get hold of a combine harvester, whatever the cost. But there are many other charges on my purse, which, God knows, is not inexhaustible, so we shall have to do without. I will ask Francey to sell us that old binder of his—it must be fourth-hand at least—and we shall have to do the threshing part with flails. Remind me to get some eelskins for the joints.

"And anyway we should have needed paraffin for the combine."

So it was decided to add a binder to the machinery in the hold, which ended by containing: one plough, two harrows, a grubber, a mowing machine, the binder, a roller, and the wheels and metal parts of a bogie. There were also the smithing tools, the metal rods, some dray wheels, and various other specimens of hardware.

These were carried in.

When the hold was full, and it contained many other matters like nails, forks, spades, shovels, screws, separator, churn, etc., the trough of the inverted barn was decked. That is to say, the actual semicylinder of the roof, now keel, was floored with planks, tongued and grooved, which would come in useful in the New World. A hole was bored in this deck, to let the pipe of the pump go down to the bilge, but, apart from this, the Ark now had a flat wooden floor, like a dance floor, instead of the barrel-shaped bottom which it had shown before.

It did not take long to do this. Mr. White had discovered when putting a new floor in his playroom some years before, that the tongue or groove of a tongue-and-groove plank has a top side and a bottom side, and, when this is discovered, it does not take long to lay floors.

The next business was to arrange about the accommodation for beasts.

It meant that the Ark had to be divided into three low decks in all, counting the hold. The deck above the hold was divided into main compartments, the after one being split by an aisle, on each side of which there were the stalls for the bulkier animals: mare, cow, sow and litter, colt and bull calf, goat and kid, ass and ass colt. The middle compartment, which filled the whole breath of the Ark, was for bags of grain, including grass seed, flour, etc. It also held the barrels of water

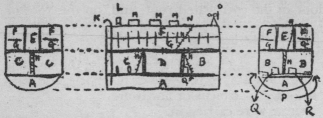

A=Farm machinery
    and hardware
B=Humans
C=Large animals
D=Grain & Water
E=Passage
F=Small animals
G=Stores
H=Ladders

K=Pump
L=Beehives
M=Spare water
N=Trap door
O=Wincharger
P=Bunks
Q=Cooker
R=Refrigerator

(tar barrels), except for the emergency store, which was lashed on the upper deck with the beehives. The forward compartment was for human use, and was to carry the electric cooker, the refrigerator, the sleeping bunks, and the stores needed on voyage—including provisions, immediate tools, and things forgotten until the last minute. There was no direct communication between the three compartments. A ladder led up from the human cabin to the deck above, and another ladder led down from that deck to the stables. The grain bunker only had a trap door in its roof. The next deck over the three compartments was divided by an aisle along its length, and, on either side of this aisle, there was a double shelf of small cabins: the bottom shelf for stores like the spare wind machine, the various seeds, the perishable machinery or tools, the medicines, binder twine, and, in fact, for most of the necessaries which could not be called hardware; the upper shelf for hutches, which contained an assortment of rabbits, foxes, small birds, and various other fauna deemed to be necessary for the future. From the aisle of this deck, a third ladder led to the trap door in the corrugated roof, and, on this roof or upper deck, there were lengths of two-by-two to which the beehives, spare water barrels, wind machine, and pump head were to be attached. All the aisles and compartments were notably low.

It took more than a day to realize these matters.

The uprights and beams were of three-by-three, the rafters of three-by-one, and the framework of the cabins on the deck below the "roof" was of two-by-two. There was a tongued-and-grooved plank floor between each deck, two in all, not counting the upper deck, which was, of course, of galvanized iron.

All the same, it was straightforward work which could be done by one person.

The ends of the main beams had to be bolted to the metal girders. This was the only real difficulty, as these girders could no longer be bored for bolts with the brace and plank, as before. There was now a metal wall by the side of each girder, which prevented the brace from revolving. Mr. White, however, managed to buy a ratchet brace, which he had always wanted to have, and which he would certainly need in the New World, and this solved the problem.

Meanwhile, it rained.

In the beginning, it rained as it always did at Burkestown, so that hardly anybody noticed that it was raining harder than before. Slowly, steadily, solidly, without emphasis, it poured on the ruined harvest and on the miserable cattle, who stood with their backs to the moisture, with lowered heads, scarcely switching their tails. Every now and then the more enterprising animals shook themselves drearily, throwing out a nimbus of small drops. Luckily the Ark was roofed with galvanized sheets, or it would have filled.

Mrs. O'Callaghan said: "The moon came in wet."

Mikey said: "That bloody Ould Moore."

Both Mikey and Mrs. O'Callaghan, by the way, believed that a person called Old Moore had private access to the intentions of the Holy Will of God about the weather, and they always consulted his publications on the subject, when it was a matter of haymaking. Mikey, however, not only believed that Old Moore could foretell the next year's weather, day by day, but he also believed that Old Moore was in control of the weather, and that he arranged it. If there came a particularly bad spell while he was pretending to dig potatoes, Mikey would thrust his fork in the ground with great disgust, exclaiming: "That bloody Ould Moore!"

"Oh, yes," said Mr. White, thinking of this, "and we must take some bags of seed potatoes. I understand that a diet of potatoes promotes fertility. At least, they say so in the Dublin zoo."

The rain pattered against the window of the playroom, slithered and skittered down the kitchen window, hummed on the galvanized Ark. It did not drum on the Ark, for that would not have been in character. Everything at Burkestown happened obliquely, by stealth. It sighed and moaned and gently roared on it, ceaselessly, by sunless day and moonless night. The ooze of the muck heap filled into a broad lake of cascara-colored misery; the beech trees showed dark patches of bad drainage in their bark; the walls of the farmhouse sucked in the saturated air like blotting paper, and transferred it, in the form of mildew, to the various pictures of the Sacred Heart.

CHAPTER
XVI

Mr. White, who now spent his evenings writing to Kew Gardens and to such places, and his mornings unpacking books on astronavigation or inoculation or whatever else the post had brought, sat by the kitchen range.

Mikey, who spent most days driving to the railway station at Cashelmor, in case some goods train might have penetrated to that outpost, which was thirty miles from Dublin, bringing a new cargo of microscopes or glass retorts for the venture, sat sunning his steaming corns at the other side of the grate.

Brownie had become psychic, and spent the evenings watching the seat of a chair from underneath.

Mrs. O'Callaghan sat upright by the kitchen table, ready to deal with the Holy Will of God.

"A washing machine!" cried Mr. White pathetically. "If you sold the farm, we could get a simply wonderful Wincharger which would work a washing machine for you, Mrs. O'Callaghan! You would pop the clothes in, with some soap—by the way, what on earth are we to do for soap?—and turn on a switch, and all your washing would be done next minute!"

Laundering was at other times a sore subject between them, because, when she washed his socks, she was by some means of her own able to shrink the feet at the first attempt, until they were less than two inches long. He had explained to her carefully that she must (1) not use boiling water, (2) not rub too hard, (3) use Lux, and (4) never try anything but rainwater. Mrs. O'Callaghan said Yes, but it was Mikey's fault for losing the bucket.

"And you could have an iron," said Mr. White, "a smoothing iron worked by electricity, so that it was hot at once!"

"Whatever will they think of next?" said Mrs. O'Callaghan.

"All these things we could have, if we had the money."

"Mikey's Ant . . ."

"Oh, God damn Mikey's Ant!" cried Mr. White, hastily bowing to Mikey and adding: "God be good to her."

It was a peculiarity of Mrs. O'Callaghan's arguments that they did not begin where they left off. She was a generalissimo who considered her soldiers dead only pro tem. For the next argument she considered them alive again, and, indeed, if any particular argument had lasted for a long time, she was apt to revive the casualties after half an hour or so, in order to use them again in the same battle. Thus Mr. White, having driven in the bastion of the Ant, outflanked the Pope after a hot engagement, and penetrated the fallibility of Archangels until he was within sight of the final redoubt, would suddenly find that the Ant had sprung up again in his rear. The arguments, like Mrs. O'Callaghan's flaps about the weather, were circular. So far as that goes, much of Mrs. O'Callaghan's life was circular.

The reason why Mikey's opinion was not asked, on the subject of selling his own farm, was that he had none. He had long ago discovered that if one had an opinion one generally had to work, to put it into practice.

"Look here," said Mr. White, "either there is going to be a Flood, or there isn't. Isn't that so?"

"It could be," said Mrs. O'Callaghan.

"If there is not going to be a Flood, why have you let me take down the Dutch barn?"

"Sure, you can take that down and welcome, Mr. White. Don't we know that a gentleman with a head like yours . . ."

"Yes, yes, yes. Leave my head out of it, for once. The point is that either there is going to be a Flood or there isn't. Now, if there isn't, it was ridiculous to take down the barn, and if there is, it is ridiculous not to sell the farm. Isn't it?"

"Is it?"

"Is what?" asked Mr. White, looking puzzled.

"Well, what you were after saying."

"Mrs. O'Callaghan, what I am trying to say is. . ."

A pausing look shot over his features, as if he had heard some distant noise.

"Sugar!" he cried. "What are we going to do for sugar? We shall have to grow sugar beet, if the climate is not suitable for sugar cane, but I believe it is difficult to extract . . . I must find out if you can pass the syrup through leather. What do they call the process?"

"Would it be tanning?"

"No, no. It has some scientific name. Various acids and things pass through leather at different speeds, so you can use it to separate them, like a filter. In any case, we were talking about selling the farm."

"But, Mr. White, you have to consider it's what the farm be's Mikey's *living*."

"The Flood . . .

"Oh, God," added he, "are we back again at the Flood? Don't you see that when the water has swept away the farm Mikey won't have a living anyway?"

"Perhaps," said Mrs. O'Callaghan reassuringly, "it won't be swep away."

"Even if it isn't . . ."

He perceived that he was losing ground. He hastily passed his hand through his hair and clutched the kitchen table, as if to maintain his position against a strong current.

"If . . ." he began faintly.

"Besides," said Mrs. O'Callaghan, "you have to ask yourself why Mikey would be selling the farm to please a Flood, when you won't be married yourself, Mr. White, in spite of all."

He stared gloomily at the table for some minutes. Then he stood up and walked over to the range, putting his hand under his whiskers to straighten his tie, but finding there was none to straighten. He said: "We will have this out, once and for all." He halted in front of the range, buttoned his waistcoat, swallowed nervously, and cleared his throat.

"Please," said Mr. White. "No, I won't begin like that.

"If" said he, "the Archangel wants me to get married, will It please come down the chimney and say so?

"Please," he added, losing his nerve.

There was an awful pause.

"There you are. It didn't come. Now will you agree to sell the farm?"

"Well!" exclaimed Mrs. O'Callaghan, overwhelmed by the gesture.

Mikey suggested suddenly: "Ask it."

"Ask what?"

"Ask what you asked before. If we are to sell the farm."

"The Archangel?"

"She would know," said Mikey. "Why wouldn't she?"

"Well . . ."

"Go on," said Mrs. O'Callaghan. "You ask."

"I think you should ask, Mrs. O'Callaghan. After all, it's your farm. . . ."

"You asked before."

"Very well," said Mr. White. "Of course, if It doesn't answer, it could be for other reasons. For instance . . ."

"Mikey and I will say the rosary while you're at her."

"No, don't. It isn't appropriate. Isn't there a Litany of St. Michael that you could say?"

"It would take you to know that, Mr. White."

"I suppose that means you don't know it. All the same, I am sure there is one. (By the way, I think the word is osmosis.) But anyway you don't know it, so it's no good. Let me see. You couldn't just pray under your breath?"

"Mikey wouldn't do it. He'd be after pretending he was, without saying a word."

"I don't know," said Mr. White pettishly, "why we have to pray at all. We didn't pray the first time. Well then, just say The Confiteor, if you must. Michael comes into that."

Mrs. O'Callaghan and Mikey sank down with their backsides toward the kitchen range, placing their elbows on the seats of their chairs, and set to work. Mr. White asked.

There was no answer.

Later, while they were discussing these mysteries, Mrs. O'Callaghan said plaintively: "Why did she have to come at us for an Ark? There's others she could have gone to, isn't there?"

CHAPTER
XVII

It was cosy working in the sheltered interior. The steady humming of the rain outside became imperceptible, forgotten like the noise of a mill, or as if one were working in a drum with constant pitch, and Mr. White hummed also, without thinking about it, in the tuneless way of people who are considering something else. "There are three lovely lassies in Bangor," he would buzz, clapping the square on the end of a piece of two-by-two to measure the mortise. "Bangor," he would repeat, five minutes later, looking round vaguely for the pencil. "Bangor," finding the pencil balanced on the handle of the saw. *"Bangor,"* drawing his last line with *brio*. Then, after sawing this way and that way, with several pauses to be sure that he was not sawing too far: "There are three lovely lassies in Bangor." A consultation between the male and female of the mortise, a long search for the pencil—which he had the habit of thrusting into his beard sometimes, as clerks put them behind their ears, and then forgetting—two or three flourishes with the saw, a thumb caressing the rough angle, and at last:

"There are three lovely lassies in Bangor,
But I am the best of them all."

Here he would fall into a subfusc drone *da capo*, lasting for about three hours, and finally altered to: "God damn this tune. *Ta-ra-rum*-tiddle-*um*-pom. *Ta-ra-rum*-tiddle-*um*-pom. Tiddle-iddle-um-*pom-pom*." The *ta-ra* part was supposed to be the trumpet voluntary which used to be attributed to Purcell. Another favorite was Tee Ree, Ree Ree Ree, Tee Ree Ree, Tee Ree Ree, Tee Ree Ree, Tee Ree Ree, Tee Ree. ("Jesu, Joy of Man's Desiring.")

Outside the Ark, things were less homely. Mikey slopped to and fro across the yard, which was mainly underwater, carrying first aid to the various cows with starts and other afflictions peculiar to Burkestown's milking system.

Outside the farm itself, outside Mr. White's humming and Mikey's slopping and Mrs. O'Callaghan's scrubbing of innumerable kitchen tables, matters were more different still.

The rain was phenomenal. The farmers, even the efficient ones, were losing their crops. It was too wet to plough. The men stayed idle, put at first to jobs of repair but finally exhausting these and still having to be paid. The Slane rose. It usually had its first flood round Christmas time, which swept away the cocks of hay that Mikey had left too long in the Slane Meadow, but this time it rose and stayed. At first the postman and other keen fishermen said it would be a grand year for the fish. Later, they began to wonder how they would get near the bed of the river at all. Mikey's cocks, and the cocks of better farmers, swirled down to Cashelmor and beyond. Dead beasts began to go down, incautious animals who had put a foot wrong. The bus service which passed near Burkestown was discontinued.

Naturally there was resentment against Mr. White.

It was well for him, they said, to scamper about

dryshod in his Ark, after putting the neighbors to inconvaynience. He was a gintleman, they said, and of course he did not care what trouble he gave to working men. But let him think that they too had to earn their livings, whatever pranks he might get up to.

Several determined attempts were made to burn the vessel to the ground, attempts which were foiled by its having been made of metal, and a regular artillery of wet bricks or mossy stones was hurled through the Burkestown windows after dark. Mr. White, who was a timorous man, happened to get interested in projectiles at this stage, and would rush out into the darkness after any unusual throw, hoping to catch the assailant and to measure the bones of his arm. This had the effect of terrifying the malcontents, and saved the farm from serious damage. He explained to Mrs. O'Callaghan that a projectile launched with velocity V at an angle of a° to the horizontal had a range of $\dfrac{V^2 \sin 2^a}{G}$, where G was the deceleration due to gravity.

Apart from the reasonable resentment of the aborigines at being subjected to a flood, there were the natural inconveniences of the flood itself. It is a curious fact that human beings, although they consider themselves to be the all-powerful lords of creation, are really comparatively feeble when matched against the forces of nature. There have been earthquakes which, in a few seconds, have been responsible for killing almost as many people as a politician has, in his whole life. In the same way, the massive facts of the Slane flood bore more heavily on the general amenities of Burkestown than the bricks which came through the windows.

The drenched hay in the river meadows was carried off in big cocks, thus depriving the local cattle of much of their winter rations. The communications between Cashelmor and Lenahan's Mill were cut by the waters, so that Father Byrne was unable to say Mass in the chapel of ease at Lenahan's Mill on Sundays, thus, except for the law of involuntary sin, condemning all the neighbors of Burkestown to eternal damnation. The farm work throughout the district was disorganized because nobody could plough, and many could not thresh the previous year's harvest, because the mill was unable to make its way through the slush. Also, the prevailing wetness of the fields which were not actually underwater made a breeding ground for the snail which harbors the liver fluke, and this meant a mortality among the sheep.

The waters rose gradually. Curlews, widgeon, teal, some mallards, and a few shovelers paddled and gabbled about, in acres of inundation which increased almost too slowly to be noticed. First one bridge and then another one became cut off. As the winter advanced, killing the last brown dregs of autumn, and as the kidney-searching knives of frost came in, there were heard the honks of wild geese over the growing fens and even the yapping notes of Bewick's swans, sounding like small dogs barking through handkerchiefs.

The Slane rose to its usual height in the Slane Meadow, capped it, and welled over into Back of Kelly's. It edged its way along the ditches, which now ran backward, invading the Avenue and the Lawn, until it was gurgling round the galvanized bottom of the Ark itself. It joined up with the brown effluents of the muck heap, surrounding Burkestown on three sides. It had a spreading, lapping texture, of small, pointed waves, like the waves in a painting of a battle at sea, with some Dutchmen, in the seventeenth century.

It was already touching the drawing-room wall— Mrs. O'Callaghan turned the photographs of de-

parted priests face downward, to escape the moisture—when the frost came, and after that the
snow.

The family was in bed when the world began to
grow white.

The O'Callaghans' bedroom was lofty, gloomy,
and slowly disintegrating. The bricks had fallen
out of the fireplace, after one of Mikey's attempts
to sweep the chimney, and an icy blast, as of the
tomb, meandered round the expanse of oilcloth,
supersaturated by contact with the spongy wallpaper, which was peeling off. There were various
pictures of Jesus Christ and others, wrinkled with
moisture, and, in the corner, there stood a ghostly
figure of the Virgin Mary, made from plaster of
Paris, three feet high. It was ghostly because Mrs.
O'Callaghan had taken it into her head to give it a
vigorous scrubbing, on one of the rare occasions
when she had spring-cleaned, and this had taken
off the paint. It had also taken off most of the left
cheek, so that the Virgin now hoved in her shad-
owy corner, chalk-white, leprous, and deliquescent.

The O'Callaghans were in bed, back to back,
covered with an inadequate blanket, and Mikey
was snoring. The structure of his nose made this a
formidable music. Mrs. O'Callaghan was awake.
Her stomach was at her.

She was lying there with her eyes shut, her false
teeth laid beside the stoup of holy water which
was kept by the bedside in case of emergency, as
gangsters keep their gats, and she was thinking
about the general situation. She was not thinking
about the Ark or the Flood or the Archangel, for
these were subjects which she preferred to dismiss
from her mind as much as possible. It seemed
safer to leave them to Mr. White. But she was
thinking about everything else.

Incidentally, it was a feature of Mrs. O'Callaghan's

method in speculation that she was unable to think about more than one thing at a time, and not very much about that. As her mind was an agile one, however, she always did think about more than one thing at a time, and this was why she was so often getting into a pickle. It was why she roasted vests, and put out sheets to dry, but left them to be rained on, and forgot that she had hung the eiderdown over the garden fence until the cows had eaten it. She had lost three eiderdowns on the same fence. Her mind was like a squirrel's. Like the squirrel, she buried her mental stores busily, and forgot where she had buried them. She did this not only with ideas, but also with real objects. While searching for keys, corkscrews, tin openers, or the bull's pedigree, in the various caches at Burkestown, it was common to find half a sardine in a tooth glass left over since Mrs. James of Ecclestown came to tea in 1939, or an unwashed tube last used for administering an enema to an expiring cow in 1918, or a dead mouse reduced to adipocere which had been hurriedly hidden in 1924 when Father Byrne arrived for a Station. In moments of exasperation Mr. White said that she was like a mouse herself, but less intelligent. He had deduced this from the fact that, when she set a mousetrap, she frequently caught herself in it.

Hail Merry fuller grace, Mrs. O'Callaghan was thinking, I ought to mind thim stockings tomorrow, they're a show, Lard swithee, it's not me fault, Mr. White, because I tole Philomena not to put on sticks, blist tart thou manx trim, it was eating the potato, and blist the fruit of thywomb, Jaysus, but if the rint and the rates was another ninety, Holy Merry Motherav God, and me a slave, pray for us now, sure, the sun rose airly this morning, an din the hourav our death, amen.

Across the landing, her lodger was also awake.

His bedroom, which was the best at Burkestown, was fifteen feet high, broad in proportion, and faced northeast. In fact, it was the same size as the drawing room underneath; but the fact of its being a bedroom made it less numerously furnished. There were only four large pictures in it. These were of: a sixteen-year-old angel giving a drink to Jesus Christ in the Garden of Gethsemane, Jesus Christ pointing at His Sacred Heart in memory of Mikey's Ant, St. Theresa with her border of roses, and a composite picture including a goblet, a candle, and various flowers and scrolls in memory of Mrs. O'Callaghan's first communion. These pictures were in oleograph and photogravure. A fifth small picture seemed to be a reproduction of a Greek icon, called *S. Maria de Perpetuo Succursu.* A sixth, very small indeed, was incorporated with the holy-water font, apparently a vernicle, and there were three plaster-of-Paris statues twelve inches high, on a soapbox with linen over it, representing the Blessed Virgin, Jesus Christ pointing away, and St. Joseph with some lilies. The roof only leaked in two places, and the rest of the room contained the bedroom furniture, early twentieth century. The brass bedstead was a double one, and on it Mrs. O'Callaghan had hung a scapular, a medallion of the Sacred Heart touched to the relics of St. Andrew in Amalfi, and the last eight years' fronds of holy palm. The wallpaper was yellowish and partly modern, showing a pattern which suggested kangaroos, machine guns, and old ladies drinking tea. It was obliterated on two of the three walls by green mildew.

Mr. White lay in this entourage with his arms round Brownie's neck.

He had decided that soap was impossible ("Soap," he had told Mrs. O'Callaghan, "is a mixture of the sodium salts of $C_{17} H_{35} COOH$, or $C_{15} H_{31} COOH$, or $C_{17} H_{33}$ COOH, and I think the right word is hydrolysis. But as we shan't have any of these anyway, we shall just have to scrub our hands with sand.") He was tired by having to think of so many things at the same time, but, being a bad sleeper, he was unable to stop thinking. He was industriously scratching Brownie's stomach with one finger, while trying to think of something else. Brownie was snoring. If he stopped scratching, which was her favorite occupation, she woke up and put a paw on the end of his nose.

When sleepless, he had a series of things which he considered, things calculated to improve the general lot of man. For instance, he had a plan for rebuilding London on the banks of the Severn in the shape of an enormous pyramid, six miles high. The pyramid was actually to span the Severn, which would carry away the drains, and it was to be made entirely of plastic glass, and it was to grow its own vegetables in plastic-glass jars on a system of hydroponics. He was not sure whether herds of cows, slung from balloons, were to be allowed to graze on the outer faces. It was to have airdromes on every floor, and it had been transferred to the Severn in order to be closer to New York. The whole point of the scheme was, however, that it would do away with railways throughout the island, because a series of slides would lead from the apex to all other similar towns. The traveler, after being taken up in a lift, would seat himself on a block of ice (to minimize heat by friction) and would slide to Birmingham, or wherever he was going, under the motive power of his own weight.

Another of Mr. White's plans was for bridging the Grand Canyon in Arizona and slinging an enormous telescope from the top, in order to observe the canals of Mars. The advantage of this plan was that the same structure could be used for mounting a fabulous pile-driving apparatus, which would smash the hardest diamond, or even make them out of carbon. For that matter, it could be used for shooting rockets at the moon—though a smoothly bored coal mine would probably make a better gun—and, once there, having vanished into the shock-absorbing volcanic ash, say, of Eratosthenes, the rocketeers would have to start blowing themselves vast bubbles of quickly drying cement, like cocoons, in which to lay down the beginnings of an atmosphere.

A third plan was connected with preserving Mr. Winston Churchill to the nation (after death). He considered that the arrangements for preserving Lenin had been bungled from start to finish, and had elaborated a system for silver plating Mr. Churchill, which can hardly be explained at present, for fear of offending living persons.

If, Mr. White was thinking, we are to assume that a coating of at least one-eighth of an inch is required in order to prevent the body from bending or snapping when moved, we must also reflect that such a coating will largely obliterate the subtler features of the face. Well then, we must raise Mr. Churchill out of the electrolytic tank after, say, fifteen minutes, until the actual face is no longer covered by the solution. We continue the plating . . .

He stopped scratching, stopped thinking, and raised himself on one elbow.

It had come so silently, so subtly, and yet, in a way, it could be heard. Blue or green or silver, or all of them, in the dim moonlight, it shuffled with tiny fluttering noises against the freezing window. It nuzzled its way for a place against the glass, making graphs between the asymptotes of wood. It threw the moon's white brightness upward to the ceiling, turning all the shadows upside down.

CHAPTER
XVIII

It snowed till January, the heaviest fall in local memory. The white drifts lay against hedges and accumulated in enclosed spaces like roads, so that it was easier to walk in the fields. Brownie scampered in it, throwing up a crystal radiance about her feet, and fell into the deep places with a surprised look, and bit them, and barked with glee. It caked on the hairs between her toes. Mrs. O'Callaghan took a grievance against it, feeling that the Ark could just as well have been arranged somewhere else, and withdrew her favor from Titsy as a reprisal against the weather. Titsy, driven out of the warm house to sleep in the frigid stillness, for not being lucky or holy any longer, mewed all night in expostulation, but in vain. Mikey sawed wood contentedly, at one log every twenty minutes, saved from having to do any real work out of doors. Mr. White exposed bread crumbs for the birds, twice a day. The aborigines hoved in the environs in a furtive manner, addressing him as Y'r Honor whenever he came in sight. It had been their habit for about three thousand years to placate whatever they feared or hated by giving it soft words, and they had come to think that Mr. White was a force to be reckoned with after all.

Several beautiful things began to happen. First the hares in the Racecourse Field went into white coats. Even the rabbits turned bluish, and there was a suspicious look about the partridges, as if they were inclined for trying the life of a ptarmigan. The stoats turned into ermines without hesitation. Wild geese became so common that even Mr. White scarcely looked up, when he heard them baying in the sunset sky. One day, while he was walking beside the unrecognizable Slane, there came a sweet, slow, straight beat of white wings close to the water, with a quacking mallard in front of it, and he went home to honey and hot buttered toast, almost afraid to say that he had seen a gyrfalcon.

The Slane was nearly half a mile wide. It touched the inverted hay barn on the one side, stretching to Mrs. Balf's greenhouse on the other, and a crunching brownness of water and ice blocks swirled down the middle.

After the snow came the frost. All the aborigines immediately shook their heads, observing that Frost Brings Rain; but in this one case they were to some extent mistaken, for the weather lasted until February. However, they were unable to be mistaken forever, since it had to rain sooner or later, and, when it did do so after a month, everybody was satisfied with the truth of the proverb.

By then, the fate of Burkestown was sealed.

The melting of the snow upcountry, where it had lain even more heavily on saturated bogs and dripping mountains, suddenly hurled a weight of water into the Slane, even in the first hour of thaw, as if a sponge had been squeezed. The river was already beyond its wildest levels from the autumn rains. Now, with a month's accumulation of snow melted in a few moments, the flood swept over the valleys and lowlands unchecked. It became vocal, slapping the hollow bottom of the Ark with a resonant murmur, chuckling against the drawing-room wall, tinkling round the last side of the farmhouse with a growing ripple. In a few hours, it was climbing the first story.

It was the signal to embark.

The work of construction, which had slacked off as it was completed, was now replaced by the feverish energy of departure. They had to make a ramp of dung, the dung heap being the nearest source of loose material, rising to the square entrance which had been left open. Up this, the unwilling beasts had to be led and driven to their pens, and, when lodged, the last plates of corrugated iron had to be bolted into place. Mrs. O'Callaghan had to be encouraged to pack her sea chest, and Mikey's. Mr. White, reflecting that he had allowed himself to take the Everyman Library, forewent the luxury of a private box. It was obvious that everything in the Ark was what he wanted to take, so it seemed unfair to have a private store as well. Besides, he could not think of anything else.

Mrs. O'Callaghan put on the clothes which she wore when she went to Dublin. These were not showy, owing to a habit which she had acquired of never putting on a new dress until two years after she had bought it. Horace recommends the author to wait seven years before publishing, and it seems an excellent rule for clothes as well as for books; but not so good a rule when extended to food and fresh vegetables, as it was, to some extent, by Mrs. O'Callaghan. She would often purchase a pound of cheese in Cashelmor, only to find that it had gone moldy before it reached the table six weeks later. She was a conservative.

Mr. White reminded her to put on the fur coat, a wedding present from her father.

Mikey polished his boots, as he was made to do on Saturday nights because of Mass on Sundays, and painfully put on one of the clean collars which were always dirty before they were fixed. He also shaved.

Mr. White assumed the costume which he had been accustomed to wear when wild fowling.

Brownie, disturbed by these preparations, ran about with a *crise des nerfs,* having every dog's instinctive dread of unexpected journeys, for fear she might be left behind.

The aborigines, now cut off from Burkestown by two hundred yards of water, knelt on the banks, howled out the rosary, and shook their fists.

The waters, spanking against the corrugated iron of the Ark, gurgling from the corners in ripples and feather marks like the herringbone tracks of steamers seen from an airplane, tugging at the wooden stakes which propped her, producing unexpected flotsam in the shape of dead collie dogs or tin cans, spread away on all sides in an abomination. They rose remorselessly up the sides of the Ark, concealing her name on its blue enamel plaque

and plucked away one prop after another. They became more silent as their power grew. Certain secret movements in the structure itself were perceived by the animal passengers before the humans noticed. Nancy, the enormous mare, stamped in her stall, making Mr. White fear for his carpentry.

Meanwhile the farmhouse had begun to disappear. Mrs. O'Callaghan had closed the doors and windows before leaving. Mr. White, suffering from the same urge, had locked the greenhouse. But the water was pervasive. In the abandoned drawing room, already filled to the height of the mantelpiece, the stuffed pheasants floated buoyantly, until, becoming waterlogged, the sodden feathers became detached from the padding and moved to the walls by capillary attraction. All the priests in their sea-shell frames sank solemnly beneath the wave, fast by their native shore. On the outside walls, the fruit trees vanished one by one: Duchess of Cornwall Peach, Brown Turkey Fig, Oullin's Golden Gage—varieties, needless to say, which had been introduced by Mr. White, and none of which had yet succeeded in fruiting. He watched them go with a pang. The wall of the horse stable, which had been threatening for ten years, fell down with a splendid spout of water.

Mrs. O'Callaghan reacted to the crisis unexpectedly. She accepted the Flood as a party for well-bred people. Every Christmas of her life, she had paid a round of invited visits to her various brothers and sisters, visits at which the large company of relations all ate turkey and plum pudding, with picric-colored jelly spread over it, in a stereotyped way, like a ballet. She now accepted the Flood as an occasion of the same sort—after all, it was a change for her, just as the Christmas visits had been—and she sat stiffly on her sea chest in the cabin, exchanging pleasantries with Mr. White, with correctness. She was calm, though sweating slightly on the sides of her nose: not because she was afraid of the Flood, but because she feared to seem unmannerly. She observed that the weather was deplorable.

Mikey was not so calm. He had noticed that there were dead animals in the Flood, and, as he was really twice as intelligent as his wife, he had put two and two together. He did not want to be a dead animal. His motto, unlike King Louis's, was "After the deluge, me." So now he leaned against the rails of the pigsty and cried as if his heart would break, the enormous tears, as big as swallow's eggs, rolling off the end of his poor red nose, and splashing on the pig.

Mr. White climbed the ladder to the trap door in the top deck, and stood there, surveying the waters.

On one side of him there was the Wincharger, mounted ready to supply their cooking with electricity; on the other side the beehives, screwed to battens of two-by-two; farther on, there were the spare tar barrels of water.

He was in search of a mate.

Such is the deviousness of human nature that, so soon as he had learned that the Archangel was not determined to see him married, he had himself begun to hanker after the holy state. He had worked very hard; he had thought of everything for posterity, or at least he had tried to do so; and here he was, sailing into the barren future, with no posterity to enjoy it. He knew, from the antics of so many sufferers who had come to his notice, that any man who allowed himself to be married by the forms of law was thereafter a trapped one, caught and manacled in a moment of insanity. It was the awful hymns of conquest, the orange blossom worn in triumph, the fatal signatures in registers, the officiating clergy in their surgeon's white, the mousetrap house, the inescapable vapors, the attrition, the alimony, the hideous vision of incompatible persons strapped back to back by law and armed against each other with the weapons of law—each, as it were, stabbing backward into the gizzard of the one to which it was strapped, with the sharp stilettos of divorce and maintenance and custody of the children—it was these things which made his blood turn to water. But, if he could have contrived to be married without falling into the hands of this two-handed engine at the door, he would have had no objection to an admiring, docile, nubile, and affectionate dependent.

The Flood was just the thing to find one in.

If he could manage to fish such a creature out of the Slane at the last moment, there were advantages which might accrue. In the first place, he would not have to be married to her—there would be nobody left to marry them; in the second place, he would be launched from the start in the position of a benefactor; and thirdly, there might be a chance of that posterity which was needed to enjoy the spare Wincharger.

For these reasons, Mr. White stood on the deck of the Ark, examining the flotsam and jetsam with a doubtful eye. He was, as Don Quixote remarked, in love: but no more than the profession of knight-errantry obliged him to be.

CHAPTER
XIX

The vessel like an elephant getting on its hind legs, lay poised on its bow for a moment, thought better of it, subsided. Two of the props, falling sideways, caught in the corrugations farther along and remained slanted. A creaking came. The lapping had given place to a fixed rustle which mixed with the creaking. All, as when an airplane leaves the bumpy ground for the security of air, fell into a kinder silence. The farmhouse wall of Burkestown, and the half-submerged cowsheds, began to revolve. Mrs. Balf's greenhouse, with its roof just showing far away, began to go round anticlockwise. These two fixed points righted themselves, began to swing in the opposite direction, righted themselves again, and began to recede. The distant, hunched, drenched figures of the aborigines raised a despairing wail of malediction. The dead dogs and tin cans ceased to swirl past, and became stationary, because the Ark was moving with them. Mrs. O'Callaghan, who had been taught the mysteries of electric stoves before embarkation, sent Mikey on deck, to ask whether their captain would like a cup of tea.

He suddenly felt empty.

He had arranged everything in advance as well as he could. Now there was nothing to do, and the situation began to lash back. He looked at the hives, at the Wincharger, the naked deck, the water barrels, the trim of his command. He had never navigated anything more massive than a punt. But he could not bring himself to go for tea.

It was nostalgia.

There was Burkestown—where he had been happy, he now realized—looking lonely among the wide waters. It was growing smaller every minute, pathetic, abandoned, doomed. He suffered an acute wave of affection for it: for the milk jug with no bottom which was kept carefully on the kitchen dresser, next to another milk jug whose broken handle had been put on upside down; for the dust-colored fox with no tail, on whose back some insect had cut a swerving path like the track of a snail; for the bat which hibernated in the dining-room curtains; for the two stuffed parakeets in fretwork frames; for all the mice in the pantry and bees in the hall and cats in the chimneys and cockroaches in the butter; for the three-legged chairs propped on boxes, and the bedroom wardrobe which had been nailed to the wall because Mrs. O'Callaghan, in trying to open its door, had once pulled it over on top of herself, and had somehow managed to shut herself up inside it, face downward, on the floor; for all the curious bric-à-brac collected and revered by Mrs. O'Callaghan, such as the frame of a 1905 bicycle given to her by her father, or half the head of a plaster crozier once used in a procession, or a plush photograph album filled with pictures of people whose names she had never known; above all, for the kindness of the O'Callaghans in that diminishing home. They had never for a moment been cross with their lodger, though he had often been cross with them.

There, in those walls, thought Mr. White, she

has injected me with at least half a million cups of tea. Think of all the meals she has cooked there, like an immense series of identical twins, only to have them consumed away, with nothing left to show for all her patient trouble. Think of her going there as Mikey's bride, so many years ago. She may not have been a genius, but she has been kind. There, in those walls, Mikey used to clean my boots on Saturday nights, never expecting to be thanked, and how many times must she have scuttled up the stairs with turf for the workroom fire. . . .

Think of all those tricks of shabby gentility with which she used to madden me. When she was giving breakfast to Father Byrne, after a Station, she used to lean forward whenever the old lobster spoke, crooking her little finger as she held the teacup, and cry, "Is that a fac?" She thought it was genteel. In 1900 or so, when she was a girl, perhaps it was genteel. Think of that young virgin in her father's boorish farm, uneducated, put upon, aflutter with dreams of dukes perhaps and of the wide world stretched before her; think of her simple arts, her hopes to better herself, her innocent and pondering attempts to learn gentility. Somebody in the hearing of that child, somebody who seemed to her to be the height of fashion, had crooked the finger, had said, "Is that a fac?" She had stored it up. She had given it, her little accomplishment, like a dog's poor trick, to Father Byrne. She had been proud of it, and a trifle nervous in case it might not quite be up to date. But of course she had been forced to put that fear away from her. She had had nothing else to substitute.

How desperately cruel life is, thought Mr. White: Life and Time. They take everything, take the soft-petaled maiden and the fashions she pondered. Fashion and slang are awful in their pathos. There are spinsters knocking about nowadays, I suppose, who cry girlishly that such and such a thing is "some stunt" and who would like to describe themselves as "flappers." In twenty years the Wrens of today will be saying "browned off" with the same cracked ring. Human beings run about like sheep, copying one another, talking the latest idiom, wearing the latest hat. And Time comes stealthily to rob them, till idiom and hat are both ridiculous, leaving nothing in the little squirrel hoard of graces.

It is not the Irish, he thought, it is the climate. It is not the fault of the race. The Irish are not lazy, not backward, not dirty, not superstitious, not cunning, not dishonest. They are as nice as anybody else. It is not them. It is the air.

It is that bloody Atlantic, said Mr. White, looking angrily in the direction of Mullingar: that's what does for us. It is those millions of square miles of water vapor pouring in from the southwest, supersaturated, bulging, colored, and weighted like lead. It is like living under a pile of wet cushions: They force us to our hands and knees. Between us and America there is nothing to discharge them. We have to bear the whole of it. We are the outpost, the bulwark which saves England from the like oppression. By the time the air reaches England, it has been sieved, milked, lightened, by the protecting highlands of the Gael. So of course they sit there, bright and breezy, and little wonder if they rule the world. But to talk about the Irish being oppressed by the Saxon in the east is nonsense—not at all, it is by the Atlantic in the west. Why, even champagne will hardly fizz here: one might as well be living down a coal mine.

I believe, he continued doubtfully, that champagne does not fizz in coal mines; but, if you take it to the top of a mountain, where the air is lighter, it fizzes so much that the whole bottle turns to froth. That is what happens if you take an Irishman away from his native hell. Here, in the oppression of the clouds, he is just a flattened Hamilton, a squashed Wellesley, or a burdened Shaw. Drop him across the channel, and immediately he boils over like a firework display. He invents quaternions or conquers Napoleon or writes *St. Joan*. And the same thing happens the other way round. Leave him in England, and Swift is the master of ministers, the friend of princes, the cynosure of wit. Drag him away to the atmospheric pressure of the County Meath, and he is only a nasty-minded, complaining parson at Laracor, and finally he goes dotty altogether, and no wonder.

What a pity it is that people will go in for racial criticism. The whole thing is perfectly simple. All human beings everywhere are more or less horrible, but they have different fashions of being it, in different places. Consequently, one notices the horribleness of foreigners without noticing one's own—which they notice—just because it is different.

But no, I won't think about horrors. There is nothing wrong with the Gael. Burkestown may have been insanitary and peculiar and lethargic and a little like Uncle Vanya, but it was not the fault of the O'Callaghans. It was those bloody clouds up there, and that bloody Atlantic spreading away to the end of the world. And the fact that the O'Callaghans were kind to me at Burkestown, that is the significant fact, that is the fact that I shall remember—that they had the energy to be kind to others, when they scarcely had enough of it to drag their own leaden bodies from one place to another, under the impending sky.

Mr. White turned round sentimentally, just in time to become aware of an oversight. He had forgotten that rivers have bridges.

CHAPTER
XX

The first bridge below the farm was called Dangan.

It carried the main road to Dublin, and was unusually high, because the banks of the river were steep at that point. At least, they were steep in comparison with the rest of the plain. They were also close together, and the trapped river, hemmed by the bottleneck, was whirling between them like a mill race. In ordinary floods the single arch of Dangan Bridge had a clearance of twenty feet; now the top of the arch was scarcely four feet above the surface.

Mr. White turned round and noticed the possibilities when the Ark was three hundred yards away. He immediately became an exile from time, so that it was impossible to say how long he stood with his mouth open. To himself it seemed a period of, say, three minutes; to an observer it might have been a matter of three-tenths of a second. A man who was blown up by a bomb in the last war, and who survived to tell the tale, found that it was impossible to compress the time between the blast and the noise into less than a thousand words.

In any case, Mr. White seized Brownie by the tail—she had been sitting on her hunkers beside him, admiring the passing scene—and threw her down the trap door to the next deck. She gave a

loud yelp of surprise and indignation; then, as
Mr. White also fell down the ladder on top of her,
examined him with a look of propitiation, in case
she had done something wrong. He said absently:
"Good little girl." He then climbed the short ladder, reopened the trap door, and looked again
toward the bridge.

It was two hundred yards away.

He ducked into the Ark, closed the trap with
care, looked round in the dim light thrown through
a crack from the electric bulb in the cabin, cursed
Brownie, regretted it, observed that she was his
sweetest heart, stood stock-still for at least a second, and made for the cabin door, striking his
head. The gangways were little more than five
feet high.

He said: "Mrs. O'Callaghan, we shall have a
bump in a minute. If you have a kettle on the
stove, take it off. Let me see. Perhaps you and
Mikey had better come up here. Come up the
ladder quickly. No hurry. Just come up quickly.
That's right. Now sit on the floor and hold one of
the uprights. I think it will be all right. I think it
will just be a bump like a bus stopping too quickly.
So you must sit down and hold on. Don't be afraid."

Mrs. O'Callaghan said: "I lef me keys on the
dresser. . . ."

Mikey howled: "Oh, Lor! What kin' of a bump?"

Mr. White said: "This ladder goes to the open
air. We must go up this if anything goes wrong,
but I don't think it will. Don't rush for it. Let me
go first, to see what is happening. It won't take a
second to get out, so it does not matter who goes
first, and I shall be quicker at opening the trap in
any case. Can you swim?"

Mrs. O'Callaghan laughed heartily.

Mikey hit her in the ribs.

"Don't ye hear . . ."

There was a crunching noise above their heads, followed by the least perceptible check in the Ark's movement. After the crunches there were several reverberating bangs, as if somebody were beating a tin drum with a sledge hammer. Then there was a sickening noise of twisting metal, accompanied by the same slight hesitation of momentum, and after that there was serene silence and ease of motion.

Mr. White, who had gathered Brownie to his arms in an exasperated way, and had even kissed her angrily on the top of the head, pushed her off his lap and stood up. He lifted the trap door, which he could do without climbing the ladder, and peeped out. There was a slight hum.

He shut the trap.

Mrs. O'Callaghan said gleefully: "Them's bees."

Long ago, indeed when Mr. White himself was in the cradle, Mrs. O'Callaghan had been a naughty little girl who chased the butterflies of human happiness with merry, extraverted fingers. She, like Philomena, had been born to a family of innumerable brothers and sisters, and she had been the Cinderella of that family. Whenever anybody had needed somebody to "put upon," she had been the one. Then she had been married to Mikey, a "made" marriage, and for the last twenty-three years she had watched her dowry melt away under his incompetence, while her brothers and sisters had purchased the farm produce at cut rates profitable to themselves. Even with Mr. White as a paying guest, the farm and the family had been a nightmare weight. She had never been clever or efficient herself, she had been married for more than twenty years to perhaps the least efficient farmer in the County Kildare, and now the whole bloody situation was going down the drain. Mrs. O'Callaghan recognized the position, and was as happy as a school of orphans set free.

Mr. White said: "Yes, it is bees."

He stood again, pausing in the strange velocity of pressed thought. He had to think about three separate things as quickly as possible—that is, before the next bridge—and each of these things had branches of its own, all of which had to be considered at once. He had a kind of momentary nobility about him, as he stood poised between the various modes of action, curiously still and balanced, Buddha-like, in the arrested moment of decision.

Dangan Bridge had squashed the bees, bent the Wincharger double, and swept away the spare supply of water.

Without bees, vegetables in the New World would have to be pollinated by hand. Without electricity, there would be no cooking on voyage. Without water . . . But it was only the spare supply.

In half an hour, perhaps in fifteen minutes, they would reach the next bridge.

He said: "Look. You and Mikey go down to the cabin. Take Brownie. Don't let her up. Have we brought any sheets?"

"Unfortunate . . ."

"There are some blankets anyway. Throw me up a blanket as you go down."

Mikey had begun howling like a lovesick dog, but much louder, and it was impossible to expect assistance from him. Mrs. O'Callaghan was willing to assist, but it was doubtful whether she could be trusted.

Mr. White changed his mind and went down the ladder after her. He fetched a hammer out of the toolbox, with a handful of mixed nails and a curious instrument of which he was fond. It was of iron, and seemed to have been part of the frame of a bed. It was shaped like this:

It was invaluable for leverages. He took the blankets from Mrs O'Callahan, giving her the hammer and the instrument. The electric light was still on. He urged her up the ladder in front of him, and, when halfway up it himself, went back to the small black panel of the Wincharger, where he disconnected the cable from the dynamo. Then he followed her up the ladder, and switched on the passage light. He conducted her to the aisle for animals, and showed her a cross-beam of two-by-two, which partly supported the smaller pens. It was ten feet long.

"Mrs. O'Callaghan, try to take this off for me. Use the claw of the hammer, or that bent thing, but try to get it off."

Then he climbed the last ladder to the deck, and looked at the two hives. They had originally been in three stories, but the one nearest to the arc of the bridge had been wholly swept away. The other still had the lowest story, where the foundations were. He threw one blanket over this. The bees were dormant on account of the weather, and, in spite of the hum, he was stung only once.

It was a principle of Mr. White's that he must never hop or flinch when stung by a bee, and this principle now stood the test. He noticed that the main hum was coming from the top story of the demolished hive, which was floating beside the Ark, upside down, carried along by the same current, with some of the water barrels which must have been improperly filled, and that the tripod of the Wincharger was bent in an arc. The fin of the vane had been twisted skew-ways; the propellers were snapped short; the nose of the dynamo was underwater, but it was impossible to guess whether it had been damaged internally. There was no time to deal with any of these.

He climbed down the ladder again, with his spare blankets, into the continuum of Mikey's wails. He dropped the blankets at the foot of the ladder and made his way to Mrs. O'Callaghan, who was doing splendid work with her beam. It turned out that she had been perfectly capable of getting it off, and had enjoyed doing so. In another minute, with his assistance, it was free.

"I want to make a rudder," he said. "Will you go down to the grain place, and take the lid off one of the tea chests? Wait a bit. This Ark is heavier than I thought. It will take some turning. Better get three lids, and that will make a ply of nine."

"Them lids . . ."

"Exactly. Too many nails. We'll take the trap door from the stables."

They had begun working like a pair of dogs, hunting well. They did not need to explain.

The trap door came off its hinges quickly, and was carried on deck with the beam, where it was nailed across the bottom of the same, to make a paddle. Druimanafferon Bridge, the next one, was not yet in sight.

He put the paddle end outboard, worked the beam of two-by-two between the legs of the Wincharger tripod, and drew it up. He had to pull the nose of the Wincharger out of the water. The tripod was now the fulcrum of a steering paddle. He pushed against it strongly, as if rowing, and the Ark began to sheer toward the distant bank with ponderous majesty.

Druimanafferon was a long humpbacked bridge

in the widest part of the river, high in the middle and low at its approaches. He hoped to be able to steer the Ark across a low side, which would be underwater, even if the hump in the middle were still a danger to navigation. He explained this to Mrs. O'Callaghan, showed her how to work the rudder, and went down for some rope, to secure it from floating away.

Mikey was moaning.

Mr. White brought up his spare blankets as well as the rope, and left them on deck. He lashed the rudder, and went down to look for some kind of boat hook, with which to reach for the floating story of the hive. Mrs. O'Callaghan had by now been stung, as she stood like Grace Darling at the tiller, and had proved shotproof.

There was nothing to use as a boat hook.

In the end, since they had plenty of time, he unshipped the tiller once more, and scraped the hive in with that. With the rescued story on deck, and a blanket over it, the tiller was replaced and lashed, still without the appearance of Driuman-afferon. Mr. White removed the blankets, put the top story on the foundations, replaced the blankets, and went down for a screwdriver. When he came back, the bridge was in sight.

He was delighted with Mrs. O'Callaghan, as well he might be, and now spoke to her in comradely fashion, as if she were a human being.

"We will steer together. I'll fix the hives when we are past. So. Push away. That's right. I never realized what a lot of momentum this Ark would have.

"A mass M," added Mr. White warmly, while Mrs. O'Callaghan laughed with glee, "moving at a velocity V, has a momentum MV."

The Ark nosed her momentous way toward the distant bank, was steadied when they judged her to be far enough from the central hump, whose whereabouts was marked by an anger in the water, for the bridge was under the surface, and was directed at the gap.

He said: "We may hit. Put your arm round me in case, and hold the tiller for dear life. We will hold each other. I wish I had not put the top story on the hive."

They did hit. The bow of the keel caught in the submerged coping of the bridge, luckily breaking it down, and the whole vessel yawed ponderously toward the bank, grinding the already loosened stones under her bottom and leaning slightly on her side; but without tipping the top off the beehive. She made a complete circle, while the rudder all but swept its helmsmen overboard, and then was free.

There was a reach below Druimanafferon where the banks were high and wooded. Mr. White remembered this as soon as they were safe—it was like a steeplechase, no time to think of the next fence until they were over the last—and he had to go below for another beam, in case they should need to fend themselves from the trees.

When he opened the trap door, it was found that Mikey had begun to scream. Locked in with himself in the half-darkness, abandoned by humankind, he had managed to stand up, howling, before they reached Druimanafferon, and had staggered away in the direction of the stables. They had bumped the bridge just as he was weeping near the missing trap door, and he had been hurled down headlong into the pigsty. The pigs were squealing too.

Mr. White loosened another piece of two-by-two—the interior was starting to disintegrate—without heeding Mikey. He was beginning to feel furious with him.

On deck, with the fender handy and Mrs. O'Callaghan keeping their vessel in the middle of the stream, he settled down to unscrew the legs of the beehive. When this was done, he wrapped the hive, top and bottom, in two blankets, and asked Mrs. O'Callaghan to leave the tiller. Between them, they managed to lower the bundle down the ladders, and to stow it in the hold for grain. Then Mrs. O'Callaghan went to rescue Mikey, and Mr. White returned to steer.

All this time, poor Brownie had been anxiously climbing up and down ladders, which was difficult, and staring at her master for instructions. She knew very well that a crisis was happening, but she did not know how to help. When he noticed her soupy eyes at last, he bent down and kissed her lovingly upon the wet, rubber nose.

CHAPTER
XXI

Life before love, however: There was no time to dally with sentiment. The circumstances of the Flood were beginning to establish themselves. It was not to take the mode of a general subsidence of the earth's crust, or not yet, at any rate, but was to begin with a welling of the rivers. This meant that the Ark would probably have to navigate the length of the Slane, which was a tributary of the Liffey; would have to enter the Liffey itself, pass through Dublin, and wallow into the Irish Sea. There, presumably, it would hang about in safety, while the crust subsided and the expected cataclysms took place.

Mr. White now had to consider the river hazards before them. He had forgotten to bring a map. He had fished the ten miles above Cashelmor for several years, before he gave up salmon fishing on the score that it was mechanical, and he was therefore acquainted with the possibilities so far as the town. Below the town, he had a fair recollection of a few miles, because the main road passed beside the river. After that, he had no idea what obstacles there were to be expected, although he had an accurate visual image of the Slane-Liffey junction on the map, and of how the Liffey then swung firmly eastward through Dublin. There were eleven bridges in Dublin itself, of which he could clearly visualize five, in their correct order. This was the extent of his knowledge as a pilot.

Between Druimanafferon and Cashelmor there were no more snags. There was only a low weir, little more than a foot high at normal levels of the river. This would now be many feet underwater, and could be neglected. In some places the river was already a mile wide, although, in other places where it had to pass between steep bluffs, it was deeper instead of wider. It had islands here and there, the remaining summits of what had once been rich land.

He reviewed these facts as rapidly as possible. He had discovered, to his surprise, that he was enjoying himself. His adrenal glands had responded to the crisis, so that he was brimming with craft and audacity. He was thinking clearly, agog with stratagems.

He could see that Cashelmor was going to be the Beecher's Brook of the expedition.

Cashelmor, like Killaloe or Trim, was one of the few remaining towns in Ireland which preserved some memorable traces of the Middle Ages. The houses huddled together with remnants of the defensive wall still standing—like Trim, it had once been one of the strongholds of the Pale— and there was a Norman castle on a motte. There were also two ruined abbeys and some monastic remains. The town stood on both banks of the river, with high stone walls falling sheer into the water, and, what was more to the purpose, the two valves of the town were connected by a handsome bridge of the fourteenth century, with three pointed arches.

In fact, it was a deathtrap for Arks.

The steep mounds which carried the castle and the abby, one on either side of the river, would prevent the waters from spreading; the high walls

and crowded houses would keep it in its course,
but like a mill race; and across the torrent would
lie the massy bridge, probably submerged to its
parapet.

He considered these facts.

He had not been to Cashelmor since the flood-
ing began, and did not know what the height of
the river would be. It seemed improbable that it
would be low enough to let the Ark pass under
the bridge, equally improbable that it would be
high enough to carry her over the bridge, and so
far as he knew, there was no way round. There
were still two hopes of safety. The bridge might
by now have been swept away; or the river might
have established an alternative course for itself,
deep enough to let the town be by-passed. In any
case, he felt able for the situation. He had been
given instructions by the Archangel Michael, which
presumably knew Its business, and that was a sufficient guarantee. All he had to do, was to do his
best. He was willing to do this, and could do no
more.

It would be impossible to judge the situation
until they were on top of it, for the river took a
bend four hundred yards above the town, which
would be invisible till then.

Mrs. O'Callaghan came on deck with a cup of
tea in each hand. She always gave him two cups of
tea, never a cup and a teapot, and this had been a
source of annoyance in the past. He now realized
for the first time that it was easier to carry two
poured cups, instead of a cup, a pot, a milk jug,
and a sugar basin. He was touched with remorse
at not having noticed this before. He was beginning to value Mrs. O'Callaghan as she deserved.

She told him that Mikey was complaining that
his neck was at him. He claimed that he had had it
broken on him, when he fell down the trap, but

Mrs. O'Callaghan doubted this, because Mikey was pettish. She did not think that people could live, not when they had their necks broken. She had put him to bed with a bottle of stout.

The stout was from Mrs. O'Callaghan's private chest, which contained: four bottles of stout, the Infant of Prague, three pairs of lace curtains wrapped round a stuffed curlew, one bottle of holy water, a photograph of a deceased bishop, two flannel nightgowns wrapped round a moldy pot of plum jam half empty, two mourning pictures of her father and mother, a satin tea cozy bought from some nuns, Old Moore's Almanac, an enamel chamber pot, some twine to tie through the dewlaps of bullocks as a specific against blackleg, some red flannel to tie round the tails of lambs as a specific against foxes, a bottle of milk of magnesia wrapped up in two changes of woolen underwear, the latest copy of St. Anthony's Annals to read on Sundays, a bottle of brandy half empty, a horseshoe, some stones and bits of iron which she had picked up on the beach at Bray, two silk cushion covers, and Mr. White's gold watch, which he had forgotten. She had, of course, known about its hiding place from the start. She had been accustomed to spy on Mr. White through keyholes: not, however, for any underhand reason, but because she found him interesting, like a bird watcher.

On the distant banks of the river, groups of aborigines were waving rags or leaping up and down as the Ark went by.

Mr. White asked her to stay on deck, and told of the troubles which were in store for them when they reached the town. He was feeling happy and capable, pleased with the rescue of the bees, and, as Mrs. O'Callaghan had long ceased to pay attention to the things he said, she was not perturbed. She went by the tone of voice.

"Mr. White will be able for it, never fear."

At this point they saw a magpie flying across the river in front of them, from left to right.

"There's a magpie!"

"Where?" she cried, looking hastily in the opposite direction.

"You saw it! I saw you see it!"

"Oh, I didn'!"

"Over there. You can see it still."

The magpie had to cross such a lot of river that it was plainly visible.

Mrs. O'Callaghan looked at it, as if she were being dragged to the stake, but said firmly: "It doesn't be any harm when they are going from lef to right."

"Last time, you told me that it was when they were going from right to left."

"Oh, *no*, Mr. White."

"Yes, you did."

"I never seed one before—not when we were together."

"What about the day we were coming from Mullingar?"

"That was a piebald pony."

"We saw a magpie too. And when I took you to Dublin to have your teeth out?"

"I don't remember."

"You do remember. And you said they had to be going from right to left."

"I thought it were a woman with red hair?"

"Women with red hair don't cross roads. They go along them."

"They could cross them, Mr. White."

"Yes, but . . ."

He stopped. He had come to realize that whenever he said "but," he had lost the battle. Mrs.

O'Callaghan must have plucked the nettle danger out of the cannon's mouth, or whatever it was. He ran over the argument mentally, to see, if possible, where he had gone astray.

"Which way," he asked craftily, "was that magpie going?"

She made secret motions with her fingers, connected with her mnemonic about the starboard and the port, and said with a sort of guilty defiance: "From right to left."

"But you just said . . ."

"From lef to right," added Mrs. O'Callaghan.

"Great Heavens!" cried Mr. White, spilling his tea . . .

But he stopped in the middle of the sentence.

They had rounded the last bend, and Cashelmor was before them. The sight was as bad as it could possibly be. There was no way round the town, and the river was level with the parapet of the bridge, in the middle of it, where it was humpbacked.

The water was flowing at speed. It was possible to realize how fast it was going only when one saw the danger bearing down.

"Well," he said. "There is nothing for it. We have got to hit. Look here, Mrs. O'Callaghan, there is going to be a bump. I want to make it as little as we can. Can you steer, while I go to the front with the beam, and try to push her off? I want you to turn her sideways at the last minute, with the rudder, while I try to push off . . . Or perhaps I had better steer . . . Or perhaps you . . . I don't know which is worst. And somebody must hold Brownie. It will knock us off our legs. . . .

"As a matter of fact," he added, "it doesn't much matter what we do. The beam will go like matchwood, and, even if we steer into the wall, to make a glancing blow, I don't know which part of this Ark is the weakest. It might be just as good to hit it end on. We ought to have made some fenders after Druimanafferon, or fetched up some empty boxes to put over the side, to take up the blow. Anyway, it doesn't matter. We can't alter it now. I think I will just steer, Mrs. O'Callaghan, and you, will you sit down on the deck and hold Brownie? Lie flat and hold her. That's right. Wedge your feet against the two-by-two. No, Brownie, darling, that's a good girl. Stay with Mrs. O'Callaghan. We are going for it now."

The infuriated water, streaked and seamed with convection currents like boiling metal, toiled between the medieval walls. It writhed itself into ropework, with an oily gleam. The walls of the passage flitted past. Mr. White threw himself again and again on the tiller—which had to be used like a paddle because it had no purchase while going downstream. The Ark moved with solemnity toward the wall, grated against it with a dreadful noise— there was a hullaballoo from Mikey in the steerage—spun round like a thing possessed, and smacked itself, sideways on, against the sunken bridge, with a shattering blow.

The helmsman fell flat.

CHAPTER
XXII

Mikey was screaming blue murder.

The piers of the bridge were wedge-shaped, to split the stream, but one of them had split the Ark instead. The whole broadside, swinging round, had struck the further pier above Mikey's bunk, rending the rivets from the sheets along a seam twelve feet long.

It was a mortal wound.

The water on the downstream side was spurting like a severed jugular on Mikey's head.

Mr. White pulled him out of the waterfall feet foremost. Like an eldetly and revolting baby with a pin in its nappies, he was making no efforts, except to howl. Like the baby, he was scarlet in the face. And, like the baby's, his idea seemed to be that if he roared loud enough at the dangerous situation, he would frighten it away.

Mr. White heaved the sobbing creature up the ladder and turned back to stare at the leak.

It was no good putting blankets in it. The water was a cataract, and the whole side was split. His face was pale.

It was not that he was afraid of being drowned. He was a stolid swimmer, like Brownie, and could easily have crossed the river at its broadest. It was the animals, the responsibility for them.

For there was no chance of getting the ones in

the stable out. He had intended, on landing in the New World, to take off a couple of corrugated sheets for their exit. Now there was no exit. The water was already up to his ankles. The pigs, the cow, the goat, the mountain of chestnut muscle called Nancy, all were doomed. He was in a rage.

There was no time to be angry.

He went up the ladder.

"Mrs. O'Callaghan, this is going to sink. How deep is the water on the bridge?"

They were sideways to the hump of the bridge, blocking the arches. The hump was a steep one, so that only the parapet in the middle was showing. The rest was under a torrent of water, six feet deep at the two ends. Neither Mikey nor Mrs. O'Callaghan would be able to wade ashore. They peered into the torrent.

"You will have to float yourselves with bits of wood. There is the tiller and the beam for fending. I will get some more."

Brownie had grown tired of seafaring, and had jumped to the parapet, to see what was on the other side.

"If the Ark goes down, climb up beside Brownie and shout for help."

He looked down the main street of Cashelmor, which was full of motionless figures watching the disaster, and vanished down the trap. He did not pay any attention to the figures, knowing that it was the aboriginal custom to leave disasters to take their course. As he disappeared, the lights went out. The water had reached the batteries.

In the darkness, he tore the beams away with his hands. They had been loosened or splintered by the jolt, and by the two pieces already taken. He kept an eye on the skylight for the first apron of water to rim it, which would be the signal to dash for life. He felt like Mikey and the baby, ready to sob with fury as he smashed the wood.

When he went up again, with sufficient to keep his passengers afloat so long as they held on, he found the party seated on the parapet. Mikey dangled his big boots on it, like the aged, aged man in Lewis Carroll, and howled between his knees. Mrs. O'Callaghan, white but determined, held Brownie by the tail, to prevent her falling off.

The Ark had not settled so much as was expected. It was to some extent impaled on the stone pier, pressed against the masonry by the pressure of water upstream, which tended to support it. The leak was on the downstream side. But the water of the river itself was rising quickly, because the Ark blocked the arches.

"Look here. I think I can get the little animals out, at any rate. She is not going to sink so soon after all. If I push the crates out of the trap door, Mrs. O'Callaghan, can you open them, and let them loose?"

"Whatever you say, Mr. White."

For twenty minutes the hutches came up, and the deck presented a curious spectacle. Ducks swam away quacking; rabbits, looking like drowned cats, went manfully off with the dog stroke; hens sat on Mikey's head; small birds flew singing; Brownie watched with delight.

"That's the lot."

The Ark was still riding well, and Mr. White stood on deck for a moment, wondering what was the next item, wondering how exactly he was to tow his passengers to dry land. He climbed beside them on the parapet, to survey the chances.

It was now, for the first time, that he was able to notice the situation in Cashelmor.

To explain this situation, which was a confused

one, it will be necessary to cast back to the time of the booing, and of Geraghty's attempt upon our hero.

Mr. White was not the kind of person who noticed what people were thinking about him, nor was he much able to judge in advance what the reaction would be to the things which he was in the habit of doing. The fact was that he was so busy thinking about important matters like the Doctrine of Original Sin, or about how to build a bathroom at Burkestown, that he had no time to think about what people were thinking about what he thought about. Consequently, he was touchingly unaware of his fame.

He had always known, for anybody would know who had been persecuted only for looking at ants, that one could not build an Ark without attracting local attention, and even, perhaps, disfavor. But he had negligently assumed that the attention was local. If he had thought of it at all, he would have said that the people who threw brickbats at the Ark were neighbors, living within the ambit of a mile.

It had been an underestimate.

Even when it had first been known that he was building the vessel, before any flood came, he had been discussed at all grocers', toss schools, kitchens, and other places of innocent gossip, within a radius of ten miles. When the Flood had come, the excitement had spread like an electric current through every market in Kildare.

People were reticent round Cashelmor. They assumed, as we have mentioned, that everybody else was thinking about what everybody else thought about them. Consequently, nobody had bothered to tell Mr. White that he was famous, for they had felt that he was sure to know. As he did not know that his own life had been attempted, he had been fairly sure not to know.

Perhaps this fame would have been of little importance in the long run, if it had not embroiled him with the Holy Roman Catholic Church. This, however, had unfortunately come to pass, when the Flood reached the proportions of a disaster.

Mr. White had foretold it, had provided against it, had seen it arrive, and it had later grown to be the greatest flood which the oldest aged pensioner in Cashelmor could remember—and this was something to be proud of, since the latter claimed to be 113, having realized the ambition of every Irishman by tricking the authorities into granting him the Pinsion when he was scarcely forty.

Mr. White's deeds, in fact, had so shone before men that they had seen his good works and had glorified his Father in heaven.

The Flood had grown to be a terror throughout the county as the devastation grew, and a faction had even sprung up, which had declared that our hero was the second Noah. The more nervous and farsighted females had presented themselves in large numbers at Cashelmor for Confession.

Now Father Byrne, who was the P.P., was a priest of the old school, with a bright scarlet face and a belly as tight as an apple. He occasionally thrashed his parishioners with a stick, in the old style, for going out courting on Sundays. It had been bad enough for him to have to struggle with seven times the usual number of confessions, worse to have heresy raising its ugly head in his own parish, and worst of all to have a presumptuous secular sage, who had not even spent the proper number of years at Maynooth, posing as the mouthpiece of Divine Providence. If there were to have been a Flood, the announcement ought to have

been made through the existing machinery, which
was Father Byrne.

The Parish Priest had consequently denounced
Mr. White from the pulpit in Cashelmor—but nobody had cared to tell the latter about this, for
fear of hurting his feelings. It had been a mild
denunciation on the whole, so far as Father Byrne's
form usually ran, but it had unluckily coincided
with an increase of the waters, before the frost.
This increase had confirmed the doubters, who
considered it a telling retort from Mr. White, and
the number of confessions had gone up instead of
diminishing. Father Byrne, exasperated beyond
endurance by what had looked like open revolt,
had uttered a second sermon some weeks later, in
which he had threatened to deprive most of his
parishioners of all the consolations of the Church,
and in which he had described Mr. White as an
Infidel, an Antichrist, and an Englishman. He
should have been more careful. The people of his
own faction could hardly have thrown more bricks
at Burkestown than they were doing already, and
the People of the Revelation had merely concluded
that Father Byrne was trying to scare Mr. White
from his own preserves. They had waited to see
which of the two wizards would prove the victor,
and the frost had happened to break next day.
The final inundation had found the miserable
town in a state of fever: cut off, by shallow water
in the fields, from all communication with the
outer world; its only telephone broken; torn by an
internal schism; and threatened by the Wrath of
God. Those who still adhered to the Romish superstition had denounced the New Believers, the
adherents of the heresiarch retorting with taunts
and menaces of destruction. Fathers had been
turned against children, husbands against wives;
Father Byrne's blood pressure, which was high,

had touched record levels, and, into this Biblical situation, our navigator had directed his thoughtless barque, on the crest of the catastrophe.

No wonder the small black figures had waved and leaped upon the banks; no wonder there had been a crowd in the main street, watching the maneuvers.

Schooled from earliest childhood by the rigid discipline of the oldest of churches, even the bravest of the Whitians, however, had required a sign.

It was vouchsafed to them.

Mr. White had been observed to seclude himself in prayer within his vessel. He had been observed to offer up a living sacrifice of ducks, rabbits, and pigeons. Even as the concourse waited for an answer, it was observed that it had come.

The glutted Slane, cut off from its last channel through the arches of the bridge by the obstacle of the Ark, rushed sideways in magnificent turbulence along the streets of Cashelmor.

CHAPTER
XXIII

He sat on the parapet and surveyed the scene. The main street was six inches deep already, and the crowd had vanished; only, however, for a moment.

In the next moment, they were back. From the upper storys of grocers' and drapers' there appeared the heads of Old Believers, showering down curses upon Mr. White, upon the day on which he was born, and the moment at which his mother had conceived him. They howled out also disjointed fragments of the rosary, while Father Byrne, standing up to his ankles on the steps of the market cross, gave forth the Litany of the Virgin and shook his fist at his rival. At the same moment, in the twinkling of an eye, the New Believers issued from the flooded basements, pushing before them tin baths, old trunks, wardrobes, water butts, and anything else that would float. They scrambled into these, bawling out to Mr. White to wait for thim, Y'r Honor, Y'r Holiness, Y'r Grace; to give thim a lift, for the love of Jaysus, Mary, and Joseph; to pity the orphans and widders, and not to hold it against thim, Y'r Eminence, who were poor, fatherless crayters that had always said the good word for Y'r Majesty, whatever that ould villyan was after schraming on his little stips. In the distance, the Garda Siochana were seen to be countermarching on the castle mound, with carbines at the ready and bayonets fixed.

All this suggested something to Mr. White's fertile mind.

"We don't need those beams. I can tow you ashore in the water barrels."

While he had been working to secure wood, and later to save the rabbits, one of the terrors of the work had been the bumps against the upstream partition, as barrels, beehives, dead cows, parts of trees, and other assorted flotsam had rammed the Ark. All these were now piling a barrier round her, further to flood the devoted purlieus of Cashelmor.

Mr. White climbed down to the deck, which still refused to sink, and extricated three tar barrels. They were part of the spare store which had been swept away by Dangan Bridge, and were too heavy to lift from the water. Fortunately the hammer was still on deck, and with this, while Mrs. O'Callaghan joined him to hold them upright, he was able to knock out the lids. The next thing was to bail them out with his tweed hat, until they were light enough to lift.

Meanwhile the devotees of Cashelmor, constantly swept back by the current flowing upstreet from the bridge end, paddled anxiously with brooms or saucepans.

Each tar barrel had a bunghole in the side, near the top. They knocked these out with the hammer, and fetched the rope which had bound the tiller. By putting the three barrels together in the shape of an ace of clubs, with the bungholes inward, it was possible to lash them together with the rope. This did not have to go round the barrels, for which it would have been too short, but could be threaded through the bungs, as if one were tying three boots together by the eyelets.

"One for you, one for Brownie, and one for Mikey. These chickens will have to perch where they can, and so must the turkey. There is some more rope below, which we used to tie the tea chests, and I will tie that round my waist. Then I will try to walk along the parapet to the street, and, if I get there, I will pull you after me. If not, we shall have to go with the stream and slant toward the bank lower down. Whatever you do, you must not let go of the rope. In fact, we will tie it to the bungholes."

"But the street be's all a river, Mr. White."

"Only a shallow one."

"You never could walk along that parapet," cried Mrs. O'Callaghan. "You will be swep away."

"I can try. I used to fish in Scotland, and I can swim. If I am swep away, you must only pull me back on the rope. I'll fetch it."

He vanished into the now slanting trap door, and appeared soon after to say: "This Ark doesn't seem to be sinking a bit. It must be caught on the bridge."

He looked at Mrs. O'Callaghan with a wild surmise, but abandoned the same at her expression.

"We can't trust it," he said regretfully. "All the same, we might be able to save Nancy. The cabin is filling with water, but there is none coming in on the stable side. There is just a chance that the partitions might act as a kind of bulkhead. If we could make a bubble of air at Nancy's end, it might keep up for her—what with being pressed against the bridge."

"Whatever you say, Mr. White."

"Give me that hammer, and we will knock the trap door off the tiller. I'll nail it back again where it came from, with a pair of blankets under it, to make the stable as airtight as we can. I still have some nails.

"I can't see an inch," he added, vanishing on his errand of mercy, while Brownie peered down distrustfully through the trap.

The converts howled desperately when their patriarch disappeared, and paddled still more vehemently against the stream. They wanted to join Mr. White; he wanted to join them. They were at cross-purposes, as usual.

Mrs. O'Callaghan examined Mikey. He was being sick. It seemed hardly possible that he could be seasick on a stone bridge, as he had been on their honeymoon to the Isle of Man, but he was. She also went below, to fetch the brandy bottle from the swirling cabin.

When Mr. White came on deck at last, the Ark was slanting more than ever. But a good sign was that the stable end was uppermost.

"That's all I can do. We shall have to put some water in these barrels, as well as ourselves, or they will be top-heavy, and their bottoms will be inclined to spread apart. It only means wet legs."

They put Mikey into one of the barrels, like the Dormouse, and experimented with his buoyancy on the upstream beam of the Ark. Mrs. O'Callaghan bailed the water in, round his trousers, while Mr. White held it steady. They counted the hatfuls.

"That will do. Put the same amount of water into yours and Brownie's. I'm going to take off my boots."

While he took them off, and his coat also, Mrs. O'Callaghan entered her own barrel and tried to entice Brownie into the other. Brownie, seeing that it contained water, was coy.

"Poor Brownie. Jump in, then. That's the best girl in all Ireland. Jump in, alannah. Poor Brownie. Good little girl."

Mr. White put her in.

He turned to survey the scene of his defeat for

the last time, knotting the rope round his waist
and wishing that Mrs. O'Callaghan would not insist on addressing Brownie as "poor." If any dog
were not "poor," it was Brownie: on the whole,
she was probably the most opulent dog in Kildare.
However, there it was. He gave the knot a last
jerk.

Mrs. O'Callaghan, following his eye from the
wrecked Ark to the bridge and back again, observed: "It does be the Holy Will of God."

Father Byrne, on the top step of the cross, started
the Seven Penitential Psalms.

The New Believers, seeing their prophet mani-
fest again, started to paddle like demons.

Mr. White started to walk along the invisible
parapet toward them.

The water hurled itself against his knees, feath-
ering into a little curl upstream of each. It grew to
his thighs, as each precarious pace diminished to a
shuffle. It could be seen that he was unable to
pass the right leg in front of the left one, because
the current pressed them together. The mill race
of water, hitherto silent there, made a harp of his
legs and roared on it. He became isolated from all
life but his own, wrapped up in the noise of his
passage.

He stopped and shouted to Mrs. O'Callaghan.
He had thought of something. She was to put his
boots and coat into the spare barrel. After shouting for a long time, he made her understand.

When he could see that it had been done, he
deliberately leaned forward into the water, saying,
inaudibly, "Aaaaah!" as the melted snow snatched
at his breath like fire, and lay flat in it, like a
swimmer, with his head upstream and his feet
against the parapet. It was the only hope of getting along, to walk in a horizontal position, as if

the current had deflected gravity from the vertical; which, indeed, it had.

Mr. White began to look ridiculous and pathetic, if not revolting, as all creatures with pelts do, when they have been soaked. His whiskers adhered to his chin. He appeared to be basking in the flood for sport, like a walrus, and making no progress at all. His movements were perverse, inefficient, broody. Nobody could see what he was about.

Quite gracefully, and apparently on purpose, as if he had just invented a new plan, he put his head underwater, erected his buttocks, waved to the spectators, turned on his back, spun round, vanished, and reappeared a moment later at the end of the rope. He had missed his footing.

Mrs. O'Callaghan began to scream for Holy Mary as the rope spun out. She grabbed it and began to pull. Instead of pulling Mr. White back to the barrels, the rope pulled the latter after him. It was tied. It was impossible to let go. In the twinkling of a second the three barrels were spinning round like a roulette wheel, in the worst of the current below the bridge. A minute later, the parapet was far behind. They were clear of Cashelmor itself, with half a mile of river on either side. Mr. White was swimming frantically for the barrels, while Mrs. O'Callaghan played him on the rope.

He had had enough of melted snow.

While Mikey and Mrs. O'Callaghan leaned away for stability, he kicked like a gaffed salmon to get aboard. He lay gasping and spitting across the sharp rim of the curve, the water streaming from his gleaming posteriors and pouring from his whiskers. Mrs. O'Callaghan grabbed him by the collar, and a last heave was made. The barrels shipped a little water but remained afloat. He dropped his legs into the cylinder and stood upright, on Brownie's tail, too exhausted even to apologize.

Mrs. O'Callaghan and Mikey stood face to face with their pilot—it was the only way to stand, unless they stood back to back—and watched him wringing out his clothes. His nose was blue; his fingers were the color of beetroot; his hair, which had once stood upright with a divine afflatus, hung about his ears like seaweed at low tide.

Mrs. O'Callaghan thoughtfully retrieved his tweed hat, which was floating beside her, and put it on his head.

Mikey pointed over her shoulder and exclaimed with real interest, quite cheerfully: "Lor! What's thim?"

Mr. White turned round in a dazed way, to look.

The New Believers, taking the tip, had reached the bridgehead and launched themselves upon the stream. Spinning round and round in their tubs or tea chests, howling out the various spiritual ejaculations of their faith, imploring the Messiah not to go without them, and fighting each other with brooms or mops or other makeshift paddles for precedence, the heretics of Cashelmor were on the trail.

CHAPTER
XXIV

Mr. White dismissed them from his mind, with anger and contempt. He had too many things to think about, without including them. He began thinking, with chattering teeth, and at the same time trying to squeeze the water out of his clothes with the edge of his hand.

Mrs. O'Callaghan had lived for twenty-three years in a fairly comfortable farmhouse, and she had paid £120 in installments on its Dutch barn. He had turned her barn upside down, filled it with the pick of the farm stock and all the implements, taken her away in it from the home in which she had lived her married life, conveyed her a distance of five miles to Cashelmor, which she could have reached more easily by a detour in the pony trap, and had finally submerged the whole contrivance in the turbulent waters of the Slane. Perhaps she might have been forgiven if she had expressed some form of displeasure at this stage, or if she had only asked ironically: "What next?" She was not like that.

Seeing his look of misery, she said, how generously: "It was Mikey's fault, the way he wouldn't give you a hand with the beehive."

Mikey exclaimed: "I would give him a hand; but it was your fault, because—because—because you lef the keys on the dresser!"

201

"I . . ."

Mr. White said: "It was n-n-n-nobody's fault. We could not have stopped it. We ought to have anchored at Burkestown until everything was p-p-p-properly s-s-s-submerged.

"That is," he added bitterly, "if anything is going to be submerged. What is one to believe? W-w-w-was it an Ar-Ar-Archangel, or w-w-w-what was it?"

"I kep your coat dry," said Mrs. O'Callaghan helpfully. She had preserved it safe in all the confusion, and the boots also, and the only thing in all the Ark which was now of any use to them was one of the few things which she had brought in her own chest, the half bottle of brandy.

"W-w-w-we can't stay for f-f-f-forty days in this thing. W-w-w-we shall have to make for the bank as soon as we c-c-can. W-w-w-why did the Archangel tell us to build an A-A-A-Ark, if it was g-g-g-going to be s-s-sunk at C-C-C-Cashelmor?"

"You had better put on the coat, or you'll catch the pneumonia."

"We havn't any p-p-p-paddles."

"Take a sup of brandy, Mr. White. It'll do ye good."

"I c-c-c-can't go into that w-w-w-water yet, till I'm w-w-w-warm again, so how are we to g-g-g-get to the b-b-b-bank?"

"And are we to?" he added, suddenly clenching his teeth, with rage against their independence. "Is it a Flood or isn't it? Are we to go ashore and go back for the Ark, or build another one, or go on in these damned barrels, or what?"

"Just what you say, Mr. White."

"O-o-o-one thing is, w-w-w-we can't go ashore w-w-w-without paddles, t-t-t-till we're out of the c-c-c-current. I t-t-t-think I'll p-p-p-put on that c-c-c-coat."

Mrs. O'Callaghan helped him to put it on, and gave him the brandy bottle.

"N-n-n-not till we're ashore. I m-m-m-may have to go into the water again, to t-t-t-tow."

"A sup can't harm ye."

"The trouble is that I don't know where we stand. Is it a Flood? Do we want to go ashore? These b-b-b-barrels . . ."

"Sit down out of the wind and hold Brownie to warm yourself. The brandy won't do ye a bit of harm."

He sat down obediently in the bilge of his barrel and swallowed half the brandy. It seemed to have no effect.

"Thim banks is all queer," observed Mikey.

They were queer because the barrels were revolving without pause, as the current spun them like corks, which made the banks revolve round Mikey in stately procession. Presently he was sick again.

My God! thought Mr. White gloomily, in his barrel—it was the brandy. The Irish! One might have known that any Ark constructed in Ireland was bound to sink. Thank the good Lord anyway, that we are away from Burkestown. Thank the Lord that I don't have to touch the door handles any more, with the tips of my fingers, for fear they may be covered with excrements. Thank the Lord that I have had my first bath for eighteen months, even if it was freezing. Thank the Lord that I can't open a bedroom drawer and find a bad egg in it, or a tin of sardines being used as a culture for microbes. Thank the Lord that the broken windows are behind us, and the leaking roof, and the crooked doors, and the general filth, and the lies, and the obstinacy, and the superstition, and the cowardly cruelty, and the utter inefficiency of everything. Yes, and thank the Lord that we're away from the necessary house which communicated directly with the well for drinking water, away from the scullery drain which carried the offals under the dairy floor and left them there, because the diggers who dug it had got tired of making it slope away.

Good God, I wonder if any living Englishman or American realizes what life in Ireland is really like? They can have no idea of it from their own lives, still less from the printed works put out by the Irish. If you have to live as the next-door neighbor of an empire, naturally you get an inferiority complex and console yourself with delusions of grandeur. Naturally you invent a lot of wonderful reasons why you are the only decent person living, and why the empire is really a scoundrel who does everything wrong. So you put out books or films which describe the noble grandeur of life on the Arran Islands, or the horrible atrocities committed by Cromwell. But Burkestown was not on the Arran Islands; we could not have obtained a pennyworth of shark oil if we had wanted to; and, as for Cromwell, he happened to take a circumbendibus round Cashelmor and was never within ten miles of it. Needless to say, they still show the tower of the abbey as having been blown up by him, all the same. It was in fact blown up by one of the O'Neills, who roasted forty of his own countrymen to death in it.

There must have been ten maids at Burkestown since I was there, ten Irish colleens. All but two were thieves. One of them got away with an eight-guinea brooch. It was the regular thing, when an Irish colleen left, to open her suitcase, extract the stolen property, and wish her the best of luck. There was no ill feeling in the matter. Two of them were in the family way. All of them were filthy, and one of them once brought me a jug of drinking water with a live fish in it. Another was coated with fleas from head to foot. They were soft-spoken, accomplished liars. They conveyed the impression of boundless virtue. Every one of them used to press down the damp salt in the saltcellar with the sticky palm of her hand, just as Swift mentions in his "Directions to Servants." The awful, the ironic fate of that satire is that the Irish have taken it seriously. They do in good earnest exactly what he told them to do in sarcasm. They leave the chamber pots in the windows and stir the fire with the bellows and blow their noses on the curtains and comb their hair in the soup and stick the butter against the walls like plaster: everything he said.

Englishmen come over to Ireland—well-meaning, kindly Englishmen, often the kind of Englishmen who have themselves been persecuted at their public schools and are consequently enemies of the normal, pro-Boers, people like that. What happens? If they stay for a week, perhaps they can go home and maintain that the Irish are God's Own People. But let them stay for five years, ten years: let them stay like me. What do they say then? What did Raleigh say, what Spenser, what Moryson? Was Raleigh a fool—who wrote all the works at present attributed to Shakespeare, while in the Tower? Was Spenser an ignorant man? Was Moryson a university don? Yes, he was. No, they were not, as the case may be. And they said, after due consideration, that the best thing would be to exterminate the Irish altogether. They were right. Yes, and if people don't say that the Irish ought to be exterminated, then the Irish exterminate them. What about Erskine Childers? He gave his life and honor to the bloody devils, and they murdered him for it. If it comes to that, look at the visiting Gael himself, look at Giraldus, who was of the same race. What does he say? That they copulate incestuously, or with beasts. Look at foreigners even. So far as that goes, look at saints: if Ireland is the Island of Saints and Scholars, as the Irish are always whining, what does St. Bernard say about the place, what St. Jerome? He says that the Irish were cannibals, and so they were. So they probably are still.

Not, continued Mr. White, thawing, that I have actually seen them eating each other, as most of the other writers on the subject seem to have done, not with my own eyes. I suppose they would try to keep it as dark as possible.

And in any case, he added, the Englishmen who settle in Ireland, the Berminghams, Burkes, Laceys, and so on, they all get just the same. It shows that the curse is in the climate, not the people.

"It is those bitches of clouds," he said aloud, looking out of his barrel—and there was Mrs. O'Callaghan's worried, loving, uncomplaining face, craning down to see if he were getting better.

He felt ashamed.

"What are we going to do, Mrs. O'Callaghan?"

"I don't rightly know."

"If," said he, taking another nip of brandy, like the greedy and despicable male baby to which he had compared poor Mikey, "if you and Mikey were to get into one barrel, and Brownie and I sat in the second, we could fill the other with water. We might last forty days, if we had water. The mayor of Cork lasted for seventy, didn't he? We should have to sit still, so as not to use up energy, and the advantage of being two in a barrel would be that we should keep each other warm. And then there was Elijah. Presumably they could arrange to have us fed by ravens—though I don't know what they would feed us on. Fish, perhaps.

Cormorants might manage something. Have you a pin?"

"Unfortunate . . ."

"In your dress somewhere. Any pin."

"I have a safetty."

"The very thing. It has a loop already, to thread the line through, and we might even be able to make two hooks, by breaking it in half. I could unravel my thick stocking, for a line. It won't be strong, but it would probably hold a herring, or a small cod. . . ."

"I don't think . . ."

"We should need bait . . .

"I remember reading somewhere," added Mr. White hopefully, "that you could catch an octopus on a piece of red flannel."

"Mikey has a flannil round his stummick, for the ripture."

"Do you think . . .?"

"It wouldn't be much," said Mrs. O'Callaghan, "not for forty days."

"No."

Mikey declared that he was dead.

"And then," added Mr. White, "we have no bees nor seeds nor anything else, to start again."

"No."

"We must give it up."

"Perhaps it would be best."

"Mrs. O'Callaghan," said Mr. White, who had taken a long time to get round to it, compared with her, "it was my fault, you know, not yours or Mikey's. I am sorry."

She blushed and bridled like a child.

"Meanwhile," he said, "we must get to the bank however we can. Perhaps I can paddle with my hat. And what are these bloody fools doing up the river?"

CHAPTER
XXV

The schismatics were making good speed in pursuit, having paddles, and it could be seen that the leading barks contained no less a contingent than Burkestown's Philomena, with all her brothers and sisters. Many of them seemed to be in an advanced state of pregnancy. Pat Geraghty was there, repentant, and so was Tommy Plunkett, and so was the postman. There were also: the postmistress, an aged and crusty hag who administered the laws of postage with the maximum severity; a professional beggar called Johnny Fitz-Gerald, who slept out, both winter and summer, except when he was in Mountjoy Prison, and who always got half a crown from Mr. White in Danegeld, whenever he met him, to keep the other beggars off; a dummy, or deaf and dumb person, who lived in some petrol tins on the public road, and had no particular name; Mrs. Ryan, a fat and good-humored grocer's wife, who was notorious for diluting her husband's merchandise; several school children, who were ready to try anything once; the Collector of Inland Revenue, who had religious mania; seven illiterates from Irishtown, who had been told that Mr. White was going to give away some money; a Protestant vicar's gardener, who had murdered his wife some fifteen years before, but had wisely disposed of her

body in the Slane before anybody could work
up the energy to prosecute him for the tort; one
of the water bailiffs, who was famous for having
got the Pinsion at the age of fifty-one; a dwarf
called Paddy Lacey, who was shunned by altar
boys; the matron of the workhouse, who had come
because she had quarreled with Father Byrne about
the chimney sweep; an old woman called Biddy
the Quart, who was the terror of the Civic Guards;
a gravedigger; three cattle dealers who happened
to be drunk; twenty-seven Fianna Fail inspectors,
who were staying in the best hotels of Cashelmor,
to inspect things; the manager of the button factory, who had grown tired of buttons; five re-
spectable farmers, who belonged to a minority
sect of dissenters and called themselves White Mice;
and the Town Clerk, who had embezzled £2,313
from the Corporation funds, and who felt that it
could not go on much longer. There were also
eight Children of Mary, with a banner, and four
members of the Men's Sodality, with a crate of
porter.

Mr. White eyed his worshipers with disfavor.

He shouted to Philomena: "What do you want?
What are you doing here?"

"Sure, we mane to folly Y'r Rivverence to the
inds of the world."

"We are not going to the ends of the world. We
are going to the nearest bank. Go away."

"Y'r Rivverence does right to be fractious wid
thim bowsies," cried Philomena, looking haughtily
upon the twenty-seven inspectors, for there was
evidently a schism among the disciples already.
"But Y'r Rivverence won't be hard on thim who
was for ye from the first, and ate the bread and
butter from yer Houly Hand."

"Nobody ever ate any bread and butter from
my hand. I don't know what the devil you are

talking about. Go away. Paddle to the bank. If you don't, you will be drowned."

"More power to de meelionair," yelled the illiterates from Irishtown, taking off their hats and wondering when the money was to be distributed.

"The sword of the Lord and of Gideon!" cried the Collector of Inland Revenue.

"Go away!" howled Mr. White. "Philomena, go away at once. Mrs. O'Callaghan is not going anywhere at all. We want to land."

"Don't we see Y'r Rivverence is after going down the river all the time?"

"It's because we have no paddle. Lend me your paddle, Philomena, and we'll lead you to the bank at once."

"Sure, Y'r Rivverence wouldn't need a paddle. Y'r Rivverence . . ."

"Give it to me this instant, or I'll excommunicate you."

"It's me paddle," wailed Philomena, backing water. "It's me oney one!"

All the disciples backed water, and began fighting among themselves, like a regatta.

Mr. White turned his back on them, and sat down in his puddle.

"Let them go to hell their own way."

He instantly leaped up again, and began shaking his fist at the congregation.

"Go away!" he screamed. "Get out of the river! Clear out! The Flood's off. Damn you, the Flood's off!"

The Inspectors gave three rousing cheers, and the Children of Mary raised their banner.

Meanwhile, as usual, there were several complications going on at the same moment. For one thing, there was the question of bridges.

Luckily for the expedition, there were only three of these left before Dublin, because the Slane flowed parallel to the main road until it took its last bend into the Liffey, along the boundary of the Phoenix Park. These bridges were not so formidable to barrels as they had been to Arks.

Mr. White was still howling to Philomena when they passed the first of the remaining obstructions. It was a miserable iron arrangement, perfectly flat, communicating between the townships of Ballynasaggart and Blood's Castle, and it was now twenty feet below the water. All they saw of it was the tops of the ash trees on the side of the road, leading down, and the tops of some sycamores plodding their way from the wide flood on the other side. The avenues were in double rank, going down and coming up, but the flotilla found no trace of the bridge itself.

The next metropolis, township, village, hide, or whatever it might have been called in Doomsday, if Doomsday had ever been extended to Kildare, was an agglomeration of corrugated iron roofs, mixed with sludged thatch, known as Nanglestown. It had panted out its lifeblood in the eighties with fifteen public and two private houses. Hardly anybody lived there any more, apart from the Civic Guards, the reduced publicans, and various inspectors of this and that. However, it still possessed a bridge. Somehow, before patriotism and inspectors had begun to pay their dividends in politics, it had seemed worth while to some deluded Victorian to build for endurance, as if posterity rather than votes were to be considered. The bridge was strong and high and calculated for the worst of floods. It had been given a clearance which would be safe for the unexpected future. It was solid and professional, a typical piece of Saxon tyranny.

Consequently, as they swirled under it, Mr. White and his shipmates were not confused by snags.

They whirled away in a bonhomous manner, praying, cursing, waving banners, drinking stout, and celebrating the freedom of the Gael.

The next bridge was equally good, and the river continued to keep everybody inexorably in the middle.

It was at Ardnasheehan.

This was also a townland of decayed splendor, which had once boasted a commodious gaol and police barracks, twenty-three public houses, and a town hall. Nobody lived there either, except the Civic Guards, who had taken the place of the policemen and had broken the windows in the gaol. They were quiet, friendly people, well aware that it was as much as their lives were worth to arrest anybody, and accustomed to walk about in a furtive way, smiling apologetically at their brothers of the general public.

One of them was standing on the bridge, with three school children, when the disciples hove in sight.

This policeman, or Civic Guard, had been recruited from an island on the west coast of Mayo, where he had been considered a bright pupil, and one who might go far. He was a charming fellow called O'Muirneachain, an open-minded, progressive person who took an interest in all sorts of out-of-the-way subjects—such as whether the tides were made by the moon, whether America was governed by Freemasonry, whether the King of England was a Jew, whether the Pope could be infallible if secretly married, whether swallows hibernated, whether Partholon was related to Adam, and if so how much, whether toads had jewels in their heads or pigeons had milk, and, indeed, in a hundred other matters which he had picked up in a lifetime of research. He was no bigot, although a good Catholic, and he had often been heard to express the opinion that the Parish Priest might not be able to cast out devils. He had always been devoted to information of any sort, so long as it were printed, and he enjoyed baffling his cronies in the barracks when off duty with accurate extracts from *The Reader's Digest, John O'London's Weekly*, the *Catholic Times, News Review*, and from any other learned publication which he was able to pick up. He knew the velocity of sound, the number of crowns worn by the Pope, the composition of M&B 693, the nature of penicillin, the speed of a jet-propelled airplane, the population of Arizona, and the difference between the Lord's Prayer as used by Catholics and by Protestants. He was fond of children, efficient, gentle, friendly, tactful—but perhaps a thought excitable. He had a soft *blas*.

At the time when Mr. White's armada sailed down upon Guard O'Muirneachain, the latter was inclined to be in an emotional state. He had been upset by the persistent and contradictory rumors of a jihad which was being preached upstream, and he was excited by the flood itself. It was a phenomenon which would be remembered by his posterity. The water was within a yard of the high bridge on which he stood. The school children were shouting, and the triple barrels of the advance guard looked like the conning tower of a submarine, to him.

Guard O'Muirneachain had been born and bred in the west of Ireland, where, as every Englishman knew, there was, during wars, practically nothing to be seen but German submarines taking on provisions. Although the Guard had never seen a real one, any more than anybody else had seen one in the West, the reputation for these machines, enjoyed by the West in London, had, as it were, echoed back from London to the West. He was in consequence a submarine fan.

He could clearly distinguish the commander of the leading U-boat, a bearded figure wearing a sola topee turned down all round, and his own wide reading had acquainted him with the appearance of the Emperor of Abyssinia. Moreover, as the armada hove in sight, the remaining inhabitants of Ardnasheehan had begun to line the bridgehead, screaming like gulls for information.

Mr. White passed first, waving his arms and screeching against the noise of the water: "Rope! A rope! Down with a rope!"

The disciples vanished under the archway one by one, exchanging loud cries with the onlookers and waving flags.

"What is it at all?"

"It be's de Flood!"

"What's on ye?"

"It's in sin ye are!"

"Flood! De Flood!"

"Down wid a rope!"

Guard O'Muirneachain loosened his revolver in the holster, thought better of it, turned pale, rolled his eyes, and sprinted for the barracks.

From thence his sergeant sent a series of telegrams, stating that Ardnasheehan had been invaded by Haile Selassie with a squadron of submarines, the invaders crying out: "Blood! Blood! Abyssinia! Down with the Pope!"

CHAPTER
XXVI

At Ballynabraggart a party of the military tried to signal to the convoy with a heliograph, but, as nobody understood the Morse code, their efforts passed without comment.

The average speed of the Slane at normal levels was two miles an hour. The flood had increased it, so that the barrels were making more than six knots. Occasionally they drifted out of the main current, were spun round in an eddy, remained bobbing for a few moments, and rejoined the ripple. The river was so wide where it was slow, and so fast where it was not wide, that there was little hope of being carried ashore.

Mr. White had been brooding.

He said suddenly: "Do you know, Mrs. O'Callaghan, everything I have done or said has been wrong, and everything you have said or done has been right? It was you who brought the brandy; it was you who refused to sell the farm, so that we shall have something to support us when the flood goes down; and it was you who denied that the Archangel was sent by the Holy Ghost."

"God bless us and save us! Sure, I never denied the Holy Ghost in the whole course of me life!"

"But you did. You said it could be the Devil."

"Oh, Mr. White! I never!"

"It was almost the first thing you said."

"You must have took me up wrong, Mr. White. Don't I know well enough that when you deny the Holy Ghost it does be the only sin which can never be forgiven?"

At this her captain's eyes began to flash. He sat up straighter in his barrel.

"Indeed?"

"When you commit the Sin against the Holy Ghost, it means damnation."

Mr. White had reverted to atheism since the wreck of the Ark, and was still promoted by brandy.

"I see. And the sin against the Holy Ghost is to deny it. Good. And what sort of thing may the Holy Ghost be, may I ask, the denial of which leads to damnation?"

"It be's a sort of dove."

"Just so. Now we are getting things clearer. I suppose the reason why you refused to sell the farm was that the Archangel had not brought a dove with it? Exactly. May I ask how you know that the Holy Ghost looks like a dove?"

"There be's a photygraph of her in the chapel, like a pigeon."

He had frequented the same chapel of ease as Mrs. O'Callaghan, in his Catholic days, and he remembered the lithograph, which was partly visible from the gallery. It showed St. Joseph and the Virgin Mary, or possibly John Baptist and some anonymous catechumen, with the Child Jesus, in the foreground, in a white shirt, looking upward at a pigeon, which was flying upside down, with a motto in its mouth, in an aureole.

"*Qui vous a mis dans cette fichue position?*" he quoted bitterly. "'*C'est le pigeon, Joseph.*' "

Mrs. O'Callaghan smiled politely.

His eyes began to swell in his head. He swallowed visibly.

"Do you seriously mean to tell me that you

believe that if a person denies the existence of a pigeon, he will be roasted in a real fire forever and ever?"

"Hell . . ."

"Oh, for God's sake don't let's start about Hell. Let's stick to the pigeon. Do you or do you not believe that a person. . . . Believe what I said?"

"I do," said Mrs. O'Callaghan firmly.

"You do. Well now, let's have it definite. Let's find out a little more about this pigeon, so that we can know what it is that we are not to deny. It flies upside down, doesn't it, and presumably there is only one of it in existence, like the phoenix. It has a motto in its mouth."

" 'This Is My Beloved Son, in Whom I Am Well Pleased.' "

"Exactly. Do you happen to know anything else about its habits? Nesting season? Song? Food? Does it fly at any particular altitude? What will happen if it collides with an airplane? When it was last seen? And so forth? And so on?"

"I suppose she flies a good way up, so that you would not see her unless she came down."

"Ten thousand feet?"

"In Heaven."

She pointed up, to show where it was.

"How high is Heaven?"

Mrs. O'Callaghan refused to be trapped into a definite figure. She suspected an ambush.

"In the stratosphere, perhaps?"

"It could be."

"Good. Now we are getting along. Now we are beginning to know where we stand. There is a certain pigeon, *Columba oenas*, which flies in the stratosphere head downward, with its wings at an angle of incidence of ninety degrees, with a piece of paper in its beak and some rays proceeding from its body in all directions, and this pigeon is known as the Holy Ghost, and anybody who refuses to believe such stuff and nonsense will forthwith be consigned to the depths of Hell, which is a place of real fire, and there he will be tortured by a benevolent deity, forever and ever and ever?"

"Well . . ."

"Is that what you believe, or isn't it?"

"She could have been carrying the paper just for the time, Mr. White. Perhaps she would not carry it always, but only for the christening."

"I suppose she wrote it with one of her own quills?" cried the patriarch passionately, kicking the barrel, so that Brownie sat up and began to bark.

"It was written by God."

"I see. A carrier pigeon, in fact. Glorious Father in Heaven, am I going mad, or are you seriously telling me that you believe all this as fact?"

"I believe in the Holy Ghost, the Houly Roman Cartholic Church, the . . . "

"I deny it!" he screamed. "I deny the whole bloody business. I deny that the Holy Ghost is a carrier pigeon. I . . . I . . .

"Sure, you don't mane it. It won't be held aginst you."

"But I do mean it. I . . ."

Mr. White suddenly fell silent, assumed the color of a duck egg with pink lines beside his nostrils, clapped one hand to his mouth, and turned his back on Mrs. O'Callaghan. Whether it was Mikey's example, or the brandy, or the uneasy motion of the barrels, or the excitement about theology, or whether it was because he had committed the unforgivable sin—whatever the reason, he spun round in the barrel just in time.

Good God, he thought, some minutes later, crouching at the bottom of the vessel, mopping his sweating brow, tasting the acid vomit in his nostrils, wishing for death, feeling the queasy lift of the river in which they bobbed, holding his eyes tight shut for fear of seeing the revolving banks, Good God, this is the last straw. Is it possible that a reasonable being ... Oh, Lord, here it comes again! Believe that a pigeon ... Nothing to come. Oh, God, oh, Montreal!"

Mrs. O'Callaghan examined him with horror. The Sin against the Holy Ghost ... But she too was suggestible. Mikey and Mr. White and the banks—they were going round queer—and that feeling and the noise he made and the way it shot out when he spun round—Houly Mary Motherav God! She produced a tiny handkerchief, turned her back with speed, rolled her eyes like a darkie, and began to spew.

Hail Houly Queen, Motherav mercy—like the time we wint to the Isle of Man for me honeymoon—hail, Our Life, Our Sweetness, and Our Hope—we had the red lobster for breakfas and I thought it were part of me stomach come up—to Thee do we cry, poor banish chillern offeve—oh, Jesus Mary, and Joseph, here's the cup o' tea—to Thee do we send up our sighs—them's the rashers—mourning an weeping—oh, Lamb of God, will I live to go troo wid it?—in this valleyotears. Turn then Most Gracious Advocate—the man in the ship said to swally a ball of malt—Thine eyes of mercy tordsus, an after this our exile—an they give me some odycolone above in the hotel—show unto us the Blessed Fruit of Thywomb—sure, there's nothing left to come but the lining—Jaysus. O clement, O loving—an in the heel of the hunt Mikey didn' know how to do it—O sweet Virgin Mary. Never will I forget me honeymoon, or this day either.

"Pray for us," exclaimed Mrs. O'Callaghan aloud, "O Houly Motheravgod."

Mikey answered faintly but automatically: *"That we may be made worthy of the promises of Christ."*

At Lenahan's Cross a contingent of three joined the disciples, paddling in a galvanized tank. Mr. White saw them out of the slit of an eye, and tried to think about them.

Not think about the water—not the barrels, how they swivel—not the banks, no, no. About something else, anything else. About the people in the tank. What think about them? How did they know to come? (It's the upper stomach. No. Keep eyes shut.) How the devil do these people communicate with one another? There are only about four telephones in Ireland, and three wireless sets, so it can't be by that. Yet they always know everything. In the war, we always heard about parachutists from the farm laborers long before they told us on the radio. Must be a sort of bush telegraph. Beating drums? But you don't hear them. Or old women waving red petticoats from tops of mountains? Semaphore? Extrasensory perception, perhaps. Carrier pigeons with rays coming out of them? (Even when there is nothing more to come from your stomach, you feel just as bad. They say you don't die of it. Might almost be glad to die. Perhaps one feels so ill before one dies that one doesn't mind doing it. Not think of it.) Something bright, something cheerful, something other . . . Oh, God, now she's started a litany.

Mrs. O'Callaghan was off with the Litany of the Blessed Virgin, to which the believers, most of whom had vomited in sympathy, were bearing faint bourdon.

> "God the Houly Ghost,"
> *"Have mercy on us."*
> ". . . Mother most amiable,"
> *"Pray for us."*

". . . Cause of our joy,"
"Pray for us."
" . . .Spiritual vessel,"
"Pray for us."
"Honourable vessel,"
"Pray for us."
"Singular vessel of devotion,"
"Pray for us."
"Ark of the Covenant . . ."

About Arks and vessels, the causes of our joy. Oh, God, I believe I am going to do it again. Think. Think. About what to try next. About getting to the bank. About when the flood goes down. About anything. Not about, not about, not about . . . Oh, I am.

"Health of the weak,"
"Pray for us."
"Comforter of the afflicted,"
"Pray for us."

To want to die, without being able.

At Brimstown a party of Civic Guards fired a volley over their heads, but nobody cared.

Crowds began to be seen, running beside them on the distant shores.

It started to rain.

CHAPTER
XXVII

The distance from Cashelmor to Dublin was thirty miles by road, but by the river it was nearer fifty.

The Ark had sailed after an early breakfast, at an average speed of six knots. By teatime they were nearing the capital.

Cut off from human intelligence by the waste of waters, exhausted by their sufferings, drenched by the downpour, foodless since breakfast, and that returned, the invaders were ignorant of developments in the outer world.

These had been noteworthy.

Father Byrne, when he had at last penetrated to the nearest working telephone, had been provoked to such a pitch of choler by the schism in his flock that his account of the morning's incidents had been inclined toward hyperbole—a figure of rhetoric which had unfortunately been mistaken for meiosis by the bishop to whom he had telephoned. The latter had been informed of the Abyssinian aggression already, as reported by Guard O'Muirneachain. The statements of the Guard, sent out under first priority to Guarda stations or barracks along the route, and confirmed by them to Dublin in return, and also distributed by them conversationally through the neighborhood of their posts, had shaken the legislature and maddened the aborigines of Kildare. These latter, from the tops of round barrows, tumuli, cairns, moat hills, and other geographical features, were furiously communicating the news to one another, by means of drums, bush telegraphs, red petticoats, carrier pigeons, extrasensory perceptions, or whatever means it was that they were accustomed to employ. At some point in the proceedings, as was inevitable, the grimly word of "parachutist" had been pronounced— apparently by spontaneous combustion. One of the two airplanes of the Irish Air Force had flown along the Slane, at a height of 15,000 feet, to escape the antiaircraft guns of Abyssinia, and had observed the conning towers. Submarines, parachutists, blackamoors, Freemasons, spies, the I.R.A., the Ku Klux Klan, Mr. Winston Churchill, escaped lunatics, communists, atheists, Black and Tans, Orangemen, and a landing of the Eskimos, had been freely reported. From coast to coast of Eriu, lighthouse keepers were peering out to sea, station masters were puzzling over telegraph forms, Guarda sergeants were issuing three rounds of ball, inspectors of this and that were gazing at the sky, museum officials were hiding the Cross of Cong, Catholic boy scouts were hitching up their little belts, typists were pattering directives, old-age pinsioners were concealing their bankbooks, members of the stock exchange were fingering grubby scapulars, and at least ten thousand of the faithful were making mental vows to advertise their thanks in the newspapers, if spared, to Blessed Oliver Plunkett, Matt Talbot, The Little Flower, St. Philomena, St. Anthony of Padua, the Infant of Prague, Our Lady of Lourdes, and to other worthies too numerous to be mentioned.

Nor was the dreadful hand of war the only threat which hung above the doomed metropolis. The Liffey, where it flowed through Dublin, was confined by masonry, and spanned by bridges. For weeks the growing flood had almost lipped the embankment; for days it had not only lipped it, but poured across the barrier at high tide. That morning, when the tide was in, the quays had been awash, the basements halfway up O'Connell Street untenable. By night, the flood still rising and the tide returned, it was feared that half the city would be underwater. The Fire Brigade, the St. John's Ambulance, the local defense force, and several sodalities, not to mention individual volunteers from all classes and creeds, were engaged, even as the might of Abyssinia came knocking at the gates, in evacuating low-lying households, warning burghers to remove their furniture upstairs, passing on the latest news about the invasion, sending each other on errands with pieces of paper marked "14.35 hrs.," and dropping in at public houses for a glass of porter. Confusion was perhaps a little worse confounded by the circumstance that many of the bridges had been renamed some years before in honor of European figures like Mr. Liam Mellowes, by a patriotic legislature determined no longer to commemorate such tyrants as Queen Victoria and Lord Sackville, who had built them. So the more elderly people who were told officially to go to Father Matthew Bridge did not know that they ought to go to Whitworth and those who were to cross by the bridge of Capel Street spent long in their search for that of Grattan.

Even the broadcasters at Radio Eireann had left their hibernaculum, had broken the usual wireless silence to advise a dignified calm. The Taoiseach, they stated, had matters well in hand.

The telephone exchange had broken down at last.

Mr. White and his disciples lolled in their singular vessels of devotion, unconscious of the crisis. Even if they had been conscious of it, they would hardly have cared. Their eyes were shut. Those of them who were still articulate were praying *sotto voce*. They took the last long bend of the Slane, where it swings between the Phoenix Park and Castleknock, turned into the swollen Liffey below the weir above Glenaulin, and the panorama of the stricken town began to spin in stately circles round them.

There was the Kingsbridge Station, one of the most handsome termini in Europe, with the bridge beside it, which had been built to commemorate a visit from King George IV—for whom they had been compelled to build a special privy also, to fit. There was the long wharfage of Messrs. Guinness, where the swans at low tide had so often snowed the mud with feathers. There, along every wall, up every side street, from every window, the crowds of Eriu stood gazing on the foe.

Because the tide was at its ebb, they cleared the bridges.

Ten thousand eyes upon them, but lost to any interest in the sensation they created, slumped in their barrels, the banner of the Children of Mary drenched and trailing in the water, the Abyssinians proceeded down the stream in various stages of prostration. Brownie alone, of all the warlike band, sat up to view the pageant with intelligent appreciation.

On the steps of Adam and Eve's, with gum boots under robes and miters all awry, the Catholic Hierarchy, hurriedly summoned from Maynooth, Armagh, Cashel, and kindred centers of devotion, attended by canopies, crucifers, little bells, and every necessary article, stood twitching and pinning and coaxing their amices, albs, girdles, maniples, stoles, chasubles, and so forth. As the invasion passed, these all, with one accord, raised their rings, croziers, crucifixes, relics, and other impedimenta, in hearty malediction of Abyssinia, parachutists, submarines, heresiarchs, and all invaders of the Sacred Isle. They knitted their enormous eyebrows, glittered their piercing eyes, propped one another up with sinewy elbows if totally infirm, rang silver bells, crossed Druid fingers, squinted, hawked, denied absolution, indited telegrams to the Cardinal Secretary, threatened the Index Expurgatorius, issued pastorals, exposed the Sacrament, rattled their censers, wriggled their toes in the gum boots to keep them warm, recited Old Moore's Almanac, proclaimed crusades against vice, blessed their burly and blunt-fingered assistants, extended ✠ an indulgence ✠ of three hundred and sixty-five (365) million (000,000) years and two and a half (2½) days to all who sincerely ✠ assisted in the Novena ✠, shifted their magic spuds from one trouser pocket to another, fidgeted, swayed, tore their lace frills on the reliquaries, shook their fists, mopped their brows, made sure that their Rolls-Royces were ready for flight if necessary, exhorted, distorted, cavorted, contorted, retorted, purported, and consorted with such an OMNIUM-DOMNIUM-NOMINY-DOMINY-RORUM-GALORUM as shook the bottle-colored skies of Bollock-Lea.

There then also, behind and to left or right of the holy Hierarchs, were ranged the loyal citizens of Black-linn, in garb of saint or scholar, the everyday inhabitants of the mother city. There were the barmaids copper and gold, there the O'Madden Burke leaning upon his umbrella, there Fr. Conmee in tolerance of invincible ignorance and the Rev. Mr. Love in hope of preferment, there Blazes Boylan the prepotent, Mulligan the medical and gentle Leopold the Sheeny with his shirt askew, not to mention Frank O'Connor in his black sombrero and Mr. Sean O'Faolain in his spectacles and Myles of the Little Horses and McBirney only forty paces from the flood. Among these alumni were crowded together a thousand priests in pursy pomposity, a thousand drovers in drouthy desperation, a thousand bullocks in blundering brutishness, a thousand maidens in mincing modishness, a thousand boozers in blubber-lipped bonhomie, and a thousand gombeenmen of every graftha, greedily groping for what they could get. There were besides: cattle dealers crafty, country cousins coy, solicitors suborned, slum dwellers spitting, undertakers unctuous, grocers grit-mixing, gamblers gloomy, beggermen blarneying, bankers abounding, T.D.'s a-toadying, D.T.'s a-dithering, T.B.'s a-phthisising, merchants at mitchery, senators senile, swindlers smiling, secret-servicemen snooping, sodalities sanctimonious, poets a-prigging, papishers a-Patering, Orangemen orgulous, and all, all, all, *ad infinitum, ad nauseam, ad aperturam, ad arbitrium, ad extremum, ad hominem, ad internecionem, ad unguem, ad utrumque paratus,* but never *ad rem,* talking, talking, talking, talking, without the slightest interest in the truth of what they said.

These patriots, upon perceiving the Armada, fell silent for a moment, then raised one unanimous howl of mutual contradiction, each man against the field.

Persons omitted from the above list included: 3aelic speakers gobbling, 3aelic Leaguers gabbing, 3aelic learners giggling, 3aelic poseurs gassing, and 99½ per cent of the whole lot remained excluded, for they could not spell a single 3.

Nor were the noble-hearted crowds and the venerable bishops the only martyrs assembled beside the banks of Anna Livia Plurabelle, now swollen to dimensions beyond the control of experts at

Nos. 29-31 Holles Street. On the contrary, the
military and naval might of Eriu, summoned by
telephone, tom-tom, telepathy, or wireless telegraph, was ranged beside the brimming verges.
There, along Wellington's and Aston's quays, the
Eirish Army with their three tanks, the men being
dressed in sea-green incorruptible, to show that
they had nothing whatever to do with England,
and had, indeed, scarcely heard of the place, stood
shyly with their Franco-Prussian rifles, simple and
decent, not knowing why they were there at all,
and ashamed to be examined. There, at Eden
Quay above the railway bridge, the Eirish Navy,
one motorboat, was limberly moored by its crew
of ex-sea scouts, the machine gun stripped for
action. Above, in the pewter sky, the two airplanes
of the Eirish Air Force, purchased from a circus,
flew round in stately majesty. They had no bombs,
but, being equipped for making advertisements
with smoke, they were carefully writing in ap-
proved Eerieish: CÉAD MÍLE FÁILTE. Luckily there
were no modifications, for which they lacked the
apparatus.

Apart from the Strong Arm, yet supplementary
to it, stood in their ordered fianna the Civil Serv-
ices of the Nation. Five thousand inspectors, five
times five thousand inspectors of inspectors, and
five times five times five thousand inspectors of
inspectors of inspectors, in geometrical progres-
sion, each wan drawing five times five times five
times five times the salary of the wan below him—
and if they did not ivery man of thim vote Up Dev
at the electhsions they might go jig for thim same
salaries begob, aye, and sorra a perch of land to
be divided betwane thim be the Land Commission—
stood solidly behind the People's Will. Typist teach-
ers, hen women, schoolmasters, bull tellers, tillage

surveyors, factory snoops: they stood at attention, shuffling their printed forms.

There were a certain number of G-men, private assassins, spies, and other ranks.

The Civic Guards were there, in splints and plasters or on crutches, earned by shyly interfering with the pleasures of the Dacent Man.

The I.R.A., with golden fainne, medals of various saints, and other insignia, stood well advanced.

The usual fairies, leprechauns and banshees mixed through the throng.

Finally, raised above them all, as was only fitting, in a wide window overlooking O'Mara's, there were ranged the Joblollies and the Panjandrums of Gangsterdom, and the Holy Will of Dev Himself, who had come in his funeral hat, looking like Don Quixote with the bellyache, to make sure that nothing could go wrong. Surrounded by his Ministers of Defense, Education, Catholic Censorship, and Daelic Revival, whose duties in the present crisis he had kindly taken over, to be certain that they should be properly carried out, he was filling in the time until the battle began by addressing the respectful crowds on the subjects of Grammar, Mathematics, the *Irish Times,* the Eirish Language, the Firbolg, How to Cure Wind in Babies, Proportional Representation, How to Plough, the Cheshire Cat, How to Knit, How to Be an Educated Man, How to Do Everything and Never Be Wrong, How to Take an Oath without Taking It, and also on the subject of English as a Badge of Slavery: by which he proved that all the inhabitants of America were slaves, because they did not talk red Indian. He was touching briefly on Brian Boru, Cu Chulainn, Cromwell, Giraldus Cambrensis, Silken Thomas, Saints Patrick, Brendan, Firman, Fiacre, and Molaise, the patriarch Noah, the Milesians, the Tuatha De Danaan, and on other recent historical characters whose politics influence the interests of the twentieth century so pervasively. He was explaining, in the simplest terms, about the bull called Laudabiliter and the Pope called Adrian IV, subjects which he had at his fingertips because he had thoroughly read at least three paragraphs in the erudite and definitive history of Ireland written by the late Mr. A. M. Sullivan, not O.M., D.Litt., M.A., nor even B.A. (*aegrotat*). He was appealing to Democracy, Neutrality, Fair Play, the Atlantic Charter, Patriotism, Civilization, Representative Government, Freedom of Speech—apart from his censorship, of course—the Sanctity of Small Nations, the Rights of Man, the Memory of Robert Emmet, the Purity of Party Politics, the Wearing of the Green, and to many kindred courts of appeal, which he was kind enough to define in simple and apprehensible terms, so that they would be within the comprehension of his meanest listener.

The cheering of the People was prodigious as he spoke. If there was wan thing, be Christ, which could be the boast of ivery man and woman there, aye, and of the babe in arms, it was that each of thim who stood to hear was still, as they had iver been, prepared to shed his neighbor's blood, to the last ball of malt, for the Glory of Poor Ould Oireland and de Mem'ry of Parnell!

The cheers died away as the Oppressors in their Battle Fleet came curtseying beneath the Metal Bridge.

The Taoiseach in his funeral hat washed his hands before the People, to show that the guilt was not on him. Then, raising one hand as a signal to the Army, and the other hand as a signal to the Navy, he proceeded in a manly yet religious tone to give out the decades of the Rosary.

The People produced their morning papers,

pocket handkerchiefs, shopping lists, and cloth caps, spread them on the ground, knelt on them with one knee, bowed their heads upon their breasts, and muttered the responses.

The Army clapped their muskets to the shoulder.

The Navy found that they had been given the wrong ammunition for the machine gun.

Mr. White opened one eye and exclaimed feebly: "Oh, God, what's happened now?"

Chapter
XXVIII

The first volley was high. It killed three publicans on the opposite bank, while seriously wounding an aged nun, who was believed to have invented barbed wire.

The second volley was found to be of blank cartridges, issued in error.

The third volley broke the portholes in the Irish Navy, which had been polished only that week.

This concluded the volleys, as there was no more ammunition. The three tanks were unsighted by the bridge.

The personnel of the Irish Navy, incensed by having had to clean the portholes for nothing, suspicious of treachery, and infuriated by the fright they had received, drew their boy-scout pocket knives and plunged into the Liffey. They were going to swim across and cut the guts out of the Army, or perish in the attempt.

The indignant populace, gazing on their dead, gave forth a mighty howl of blended origins, including the curse of the gravecloth, the caointeachán, the battle cry (Bollock-Lea Aboo), and the appeal for quarter.

Then, as the blue smoke drifted on the wintry air and the sea gulls which had risen at the crash of ordnance settled down once more, the emotional solution crystallized in the twinkling of an eye. The bishops began to lay about them with their croziers, the inspectors slapped each other with their notebooks, the remaining publicans crowned each other with empty bottles, the black-coated workers belabored each other with umbrellas, the shopkeepers exchanged rotten eggs and cabbage stumps, the Army clubbed their harquebuses and fought off the Navy, the St. John's ambulances rang their bells, the Fire Brigade turned on their hoses, which were found to have perished, the Gaelic Leaguers slashed each other with genuine shillelaghs, the banshees bawled, the leprechauns lepped, the I.R.A. discharged their tommy guns, the D.T.'s went for the T.D.'s, the mincing maidens stabbed each other with safety pins, the bullocks bolted, the drovers slogged each other with their ash plants, the slum dwellers smashed the shop windows and began to loot, Mr. Bloom withdrew, Blazes Boylan gave Mulligan the medical a black eye, the pursy priests blew out their cheeks and assaulted each other with their breviaries, the Civic Guards were massacred to a man, and the Boss in his bow window overlooking O'Mara's delivered an instructive address in Daelic on the iniquitous behavior of King Henry II.

The last of the invaders, as they shot under Butt Bridge toward the Customs House, turned back a weary eye.

The stricken city stretched behind them in three layers. The upper and missile layer was of bowler hats, boots, bricks, books, bottles, and other bric-a-brac, which were tossed up and down in the afflatus of the crowd, like balls on a fountain at a fair. The second or striking layer rose and fell in a continuous twinkle, and consisted of walking sticks, wands, umbrellas, clubs, whisky bottles, truncheons, shillelaghs, rails, pokers, hurleys, bludgeons, tram rails, coshes. The third layer was black, confused, hideous, interwoven, writhing, tightly packed, desperate, and snarling. It seemed to be human, but roared like the great cats at feeding time. And wounding, hurting, blood-dripping, savage, gory, sharp-edged, strong-grasping, red-faced, swiftsmiting, vast, wild, ill-fated was their combat on both sides.

Long afterward, Mrs. O'Callaghan said: "I found . . . me keys."

Mikey asked: "Where?"

"In me . . . pocket."

They waltzed past the North Wall and the entrance to the Grand Canal Dock. Lighthouses began to show unlighted in the downpour, and, on their right, the Pigeon House Road stretched its long length just level with the water. The Isolation Hospital and the Main Drainage Outfall, the Lifeboat House and the streaming Pigeon House itself, lastly the Electricity Works, they bade them a long farewell.

Mr. White asked: "Did you see . . . all those people?"

"They was . . . shooting at us."

"Nonsense."

On their left there were two beacons bobbing, on their right the endless pier to Poolbeg Lighthouse. They were almost at sea, and it was rougher.

"Why . . . should they?"

"Perhaps . . . we done wrong."

"If they shot," said Mr. White wanly, holding his collar with a weak hand against the rain, "they must have been shooting at each other. Perhaps there is a revolution. They generally have one . . . about Easter."

Behind them the last roars of the multitude were blended to a stilly hum. The raindrops on the water round them rose in a million pawns.

"They must have . . . seen us?"

There was no answer.

"Surely they will send . . .a boat?"

Silence.

Between the Poolbeg and the North Bull lights the sea took over.

The barrels rose with the blasts from the harbor and the haven out over the ridge fences of the floodlike, strange, wonderful, noisy-bordered, generous, broad, ever rough, wet-hollowed, shower-dewy, loud-graveled, full-streamed salt ocean; so that the sea rose in its blue-gray, sudden, hideous surface, and in its unhindered mad brinks, and in its powerful, strong-noisy, swift-abusive, fish-fruitful waves; so that the noise of the immense sea, and the tumult of the violence, and the rough clamor of the sea monsters would be heard on every side, in their necessity and oppression.

The disciples had lost their paddles when they had started to be sick.

The current of the river died away. The currents of the Eirish Ocean carried them heaving southward. They rose high to the heavens, elevated as a sacrifice, and were plunged down, down, into the abyss. Ducks of the sea, flying along the surface, vanished behind the waves and rose again, an agony to witness. Their straight lines emphasized the curves.

Mrs. O'Callaghan said: "It could be . . . a special kine of a bird. Like the pemmican."

"What could?"

"The Houly Ghost."

Mikey said bitterly: "Thim bowzies. They only have her for the orferings."

"Mikey!"

"A pun note at Easter, an' a pun note at Candlemas, an' a pun note at Hallowe'en, an' a pun note at Chrissymas."

He looked over the rim of his barrel and added

with anxiety: "Oh, Lor! Will thim waves come in?"

"Probably."

"We won't float then."

"No."

"We'll be drownded."

"Yes."

"Whoooo. . . ."

Mrs. O'Callaghan started an Act of Contrition.

It was seen that Philomena's brothers and sisters had produced twenty-three colored cravats, once the property of Mr. White, and were waving them feebly on the crests. At the next crest they saw the reason.

The mail boat from England, on her daily beeline from Holyhead, under her accustomed plume of smoke, was treading the last lap.

Mrs. O'Callaghan waved her keys.

Mr. White refused to look.

"They won't see us."

The steamer unbelievably turned, made toward them, began to slow. It came close. People stood along the rails and began throwing life belts at them: dangerous weapons, and deprecated by the Captain, who did not want to have them lost. A boat was lowered on creaking blocks, the first time it had been moved for generations. The sailors, who had the faint air of being railway porters which seems peculiar to the Eirish passage, seemed surprised to see it work. The cliff of the ship's side towered over the navigators, who now, reacting to their rescue, were seen to be in a state of collapse. Sympathetic passengers also threw ropes at them, wherever they found them coiled up, and a few threw fire buckets. The people from the bar began throwing bottles. Many took photographs. Stewardesses constructed stretchers, filled hot-water jars, prepared Benger's Food. The lifeboat was found to be seaworthy, was manned, disentangled from its davits, and rowed among the castaways. Muscular seamen with gentle hands hauled them across the gunwales, out of their tubs and tanks. They were dragged on board in one way and another, with lolling heads and cadaverous faces, each patient with an arm round two men's necks. They were safe, and to some extent grateful. Rum was issued. Even the rain began to clear.

Mr. White and his party were the last to come aboard, the former making sure that Brownie would be safe. She bounded round them on the deck.

They stood for a short time with a man on either side, while some argument was made about a cabin. The mail boat did not bounce so much as the barrels, and it was a relief not to be turning round. He trusted himself to open half an eye.

Over Eireland the sun was drooping. Bray Head stood up in lovely purple under the slanting beams, and the still hush of evening ushered the last long veil of rain away.

He could be seen to be beckoning to Mrs. O'Callaghan, nodding feebly, pointing to the starboard with a bluish claw. She looked along it obediently, confused, co-operative, unconquered. She smiled her ghostly smile of manners, the one which she used for Father Byrne when she said, "Is that a fac?", to show that she had seen it too.

They were carried swaying to their bunks.

It was a perfect rainbow.

In the vast intergalactic world of the future
the soldiers battle

NOT FOR GLORY

JOEL ROSENBERG

author of the bestselling
Guardian of the Flame series

Only once in the history of the Metzadan merce-
nary corps has a man been branded traitor. That
man is Bar-El, the most cunning military mind in
the universe. Now his nephew, Inspector-General
Hanavi, must turn to him for help. What begins as
one final mission is transformed into a series of
campaigns that takes the Metzadans from world to
world, into intrigues, dangers, and treacherous dip-
lomatic games, where a strategist's highly irregu-
lar maneuvers and a master assassin's swift blade
may prove the salvation of the planet—or its ulti-
mate ruin . . .